PRAISE FOR JAN KOZLOWSKI'S
DIE, YOU BASTARD! DIE!

"Although I care little whether great books come from a man or a woman, I can honestly say I'd been waiting for something like *Die, You Bastard! Die!* from a female author. The list of hardcore horror masters is full of men, and Kozlowski is now in there with the best of them. Between the clean, concise writing and the unexpected plot twists and unfiltered sadism – from little girls being forced to take their "medicine" and the anger that comes from reading about abuse to the power of revenge and a guy being turned into a cockroach piñata – Kozlowski shows that she's not afraid to tackle anything and has the chops to do it successfully."
– Gabino Iglesias, *HorrorTalk*

"Kozlowski's prose is horrifying in its directness and detail, a fast-paced gut punch that will leave you reeling. I absolutely loved this book."
– *The Horror Fiction Review*

"Human monsters don't get more humanly monstrous than Big Daddy. And it don't get much rougher and tougher than Jan Kozlowski's violently matter-of-fact, emotionally ass-kicking, downright inceniary son of a bitch."
-- John Skipp (from the original intro)

DIE, YOU BASTARD! DIE!

JAN KOZLOWSKI

DEADITE PRESS
P.O. BOX 10065
PORTLAND, OR 97296
WWW.ERASERHEADPRESS.COM

ISBN: 978-1-62105-180-0

For my husband, Peter

CHAPTER ONE

The orange and white Albany County ambulance cruised down Western Avenue, past the Georgian brick buildings and the green copper cupola that marked the heart of the SUNY Downtown campus. Paramedic Claire Valentin's trained eyes scanned the parking lots, sidewalks and paths, searching for possible candidates. This was usually a pretty target-rich environment. The weather was per- fect, bright and clear, with just the slightest tang of lingering winter chill. She checked her watch; it was the perfect time of day, too.

"Bogie at ten o'clock, Claire."

"Beautiful, I see her. Wow, she's a busy little multi-tasker, isn't she? Sidewalks on both sides of the street but she's jogging in the road with a stroller, a dog on a leash, *and* a cell phone plastered to her ear. Follow her down South Lake, nice and slow."

The ambulance turned left at the Adventist church and settled in about a car's length behind the woman and her entourage. By the time they had passed Thurlow Terrace, the jogger noticed them and moved over closer to the sidewalk, presumably so they could pass. When they were still hanging with her after she passed New Scotland Avenue, she took her hand off the stroller and motioned them past. When they didn't respond, she continued running for another block, but put away the cell and kept glancing back at them. At the corner of South Lake and Madison, she moved up onto the sidewalk and turned to glare at them.

"What's going on? Why are you following me?" the jogger demanded as Jim rolled to a stop next to her.

"Well Ma'am," he drawled. "We were driving past and we no- ticed you, your dog, your baby and your cell phone bouncing down the middle of a city street. We knew it would only be a matter of time before we'd be getting a call to scrape your mangled bodies off the pavement, so we figured we might as well save the gas and just slide in behind you and wait."

"Well, I never...Who do you think you...I have every right..."

"Yes Ma'am, that's what's so great about this country of ours. We all have the right to be as self-absorbed, reckless and stupidas we can possibly be. And frankly, that's a big part of what keeps ambulance companies, hospitals and funeral parlors in business. You have yourself a nice day, now."

"Ah, I love it when you leave them speechless," Claire said as they pulled away from the open-mouthed woman and rejoined the flow of traffic.

"What can I say? I learned from the master. Remember the guy who was walking down Central Avenue reading that big old Stephen King hardback? I thought you were going to make him eat that thing one page at a time."

"Yeah, I was surprised we never got into any trouble over that one. He seemed like the call and complain type."

"I don't know, I recall you threatening to turn that best seller into a suppository if he ever, under any circumstances, crossed your path again. I have the feeling he believed you."

"Well, we of the Street Smarts Division of the Rolling Educational Ministry can only hope. Isn't that right, Brother Jim?"

"Hallelujah Sister Cl..."

"Albany police dispatch to Paramedic car 45."

CHAPTER TWO

"45."

"Car 45, respond to 863 Myrtle Ave for a sick child. No details, but the caller sounded distraught, so take it on a priority one just in case. Patrol car is enroute."

"10-4, Car 45 responding." Claire hung up the mike and worked the lights and sirens while Jim maneuvered them through traffic.

"Damn, I hate the 800 block of Myrtle," Jim said. "Every freaking house has a mile long set of stone steps, and it's always the only way in. One of these days, you, me and the patient are go- ing to end up splattered at the bottom of one of them, just like that priest in *The Exorcist*."

"Dimmy...why you do this to me, Dimmy?" Claire quoted.

"Your mother sucks cock in Hell, Karras," Jim countered.

"All right, yours is better. First point in today's Movie Quote War goes to Aurelio. Okay, we're on Myrtle. Let's get a number. I've got 917, slow down."

"There it is, 863, the house with the blue second floor."

"Albany PD, Car 45 arrival 863 Myrtle."

"10-4, Car 45."

"Is APD meeting us?" Claire asked.

"10-4, but it'll be a few minutes. Advise you wait for APD back up before entering the scene."

"10-4." Claire already had the door open and was halfway out of it.

"10-4 my ass," Jim said, picking the mike up off the floor where she had thrown it. "You're going up there, aren't you?"

"Nah...I'm just going to take a quick look around. The call was for a sick kid. It's probably just a baby with a cold and a new momma who doesn't know which end to diaper yet. You stay here and flag down the cops and I'll..."

"Oh no you won't. You know the rule. If you go, I go."

"All right, let's see what's going on, then." Claire grabbed the jump kit, and they hit the long flight of cement steps that led to yet another flight of wooden porch stairs.

"Do you want to bet these aren't the last stairs we see on this call?"

"No bet. Inverse law of EMS, the size of the patient is always inversely relational to the number of stairs you have to traverse."

"Hey, even an 800lb 50 year old is somebody's 'baby'. No one said for sure this was a pediatric call."

"Thanks. You are a font of optimism this morning."

They crossed the wide porch and, out of habit, flattened themselves on either side of the door before knocking loudly. Claire's second day on the job, eighteen plus years ago, she had seen a shotgun hole blown through a door just like this one. You only have to see one to forever break you of walking up to a door straight on.

"Ambulance!" she called out.

"Yes, coming," a muffled female voice responded. Footsteps approached the door, followed by the clunking of locks turning. "Thank God you're here. My baby..."

The woman that answered the door was covered in blood. Not light sprays or splatters, not a mist or drops, but dripping head to toe in thick, dark, chunky sauce, like Carrie on prom night.

Claire dropped her kit on the porch. "Ma'am, are you all right?"

"Oh, this..." the woman answered, looking down at herself. "Don't worry, this isn't mine. Please, my little girl is in the back. I don't think she's breathing. Please help her." She turned and disappeared into the interior of the house.

"Jim, get APD. Tell them to move it."

"Claire, don't go in there. You don't know..."

"No choice. Get APD and I'll check on the kid. Please. Now."

"I'm calling on the cell. I'll be right behind you."

Claire followed the woman through the fairly neat living room and kitchen. It looked homey and comfortable, except for the bloody footprints that crisscrossed the rugs and linoleum. Beyond the kitchen, there was a hallway with three doors. The woman led her to the last door, the only open one, and pointed her to the bed where the blond head of a small girl poked out from underneath the naked, bloody, and apparently unconscious mountain of a man.

"What happened here, Ma'am?" Claire asked as she rushed forward and tried to feel a pulse in the girl's neck. There was something there. It was hard to catch under the circumstances, but she had a pulse.

"Jim! Get the oxygen and a basket, we're going to scoop and screw with the kid. Tell dispatch to get another crew in here priority one for a second patient, an adult male." She took a quick body survey. "Tell them he's got a thready pulse and he's breathing, but it looks like Cheyne-Stokes respirations secondary to traumatic brain injury. Ma'am, you were telling me what happened?"

"I came home from work early. I work third shift at the 24-hour convenience out by the mall. I wasn't feeling good and I got Shirleen to come in early for me. I got home and Bethie wasn't in her bed, so I went in to ask George where she was and...and...he was passed out, *naked* and on top of her and she wasn't moving. I...I...grabbed the first thing I saw, and I started hitting him with it, trying to get him off of her, trying to hurt him and make him move. Then there was blood, so much blood, and it made him even slip- perier and harder to move, and I kept hitting him. I got him rolled off her a little, and that's when I called 911 and you came. Is she breathing? Is she alive?"

"Yes Ma'am, she's got a pulse. Can you tell me how old she is?"

"She's only four...she just turned four last week."

Jim and three officers appeared in the doorway. "Guys, help me move him. We've got to get the girl out from underneath him, *now*!"

The four men dug rubber gloves out of their pockets and waded in.

"Valentin, at least try to keep it somewhere in the forefront of that beautiful mind of yours that this is a crime scene," the sergeant whispered in her ear as they sorted themselves into position to lift the man's body.

"Yeah, it's a real mystery, all right. And isn't that just like a male, just assuming that your needs always have to come first."

"Whooo, what's a matter, Valentin? Your time of the month, or you just feeling a little more femi-Nazi than usual today?"

"Bite me, Sarge. And while you're at it, *lift!*"

As soon as she saw a sliver of daylight between the two bodies, Claire grabbed the little girl by her shoulders and pulled her forward. Jim angled his long, skinny frame between Claire, the cops, the fat guy and the child and snapped the two halves of the rescue basket into place around the patient. Claire grabbed one end and Jim the other, and they slid her off the bed in one smooth motion.

"Okay, we got her. Lower him back down, nice and easy. Try not to move him around too much. And if any of you guys have an oxygen tank and mask in the back of your cruiser, it wouldn't hurt to slap it on him until the other crew gets here. They're en route. It should only be a couple of minutes."

They set the metal stretcher down long enough to slip an oxygen mask over the child's face, cover her naked body with a clean sheet, and take another quick pulse reading. Their eyes met over the kid's head. "We've got to go, Claire." Jim said.

"Ma'am, we're taking her to Pine Hills Hospital. Is Bethie allergic to anything?"

"No, nothing. I'm coming with her. I have to be with her." Claire saw the Sergeant standing behind the mother, shaking

his head. More police began to fill the room. "The police will bring you along in a few minutes. They just have a few questions for you first."

"No, *no*!"

"Claire, we have to go."

CHAPTER THREE

Jim and Claire hustled their patient down the multiple flights of stairs and out to the ambulance. They did a quick body survey, got another set of vitals, adjusted her oxygen levels and prepared to transport. Pine Hills was less than a mile away, and sometimes the best thing you could do for your patient was to get them to the Emergency Department as soon as possible.

Claire gave them a quick radio call to let them know what they were coming in with and what their ETA was. When they landed on their doorstep two minutes later, it seemed like half the E.D. was waiting for them. Surrounded by a sea of green scrubs and security uniforms, they rolled Bethie out of the back of the ambu- lance and straight into Trauma Room #2.

Medical professionals were a hard-nosed bunch, but kiddy calls were everyone's Achilles. Nurses, docs, paramedics and techs that normally didn't bat an eyelash at the gore-encrusted results of the motor vehicle accidents, gang wars and the other acts of human stupidity that paraded through their work days, would go to pieces after a bad pediatric call.

Claire turned her patient over to the E.D. team and left the room. Normally, she'd stay for a few minutes to watch the doctors and nurses work, or at least to retrieve her equipment, but she could feel the neck of her uniform getting tight and that ooochie feeling crawling up between her shoulder blades. She grabbed an empty chair at the nurse's station, took a few deep breaths and tried to focus on her paperwork.

Fifteen minutes later, she was still sitting there, trying to collect her thoughts enough to write her report, when the E.D.'s radio went off. Car 52 was on their way in with the second patient from the Myrtle St. scene. Outstanding, Claire thought. The pervert's going to end up in the same trauma suite as his victim. And worse, the E.D. staff will be obligated to work just as hard to save his miserable life as they were to save Bethie's. No expense will be spared, no favoritism or judgment allowed. Everyone has rights, and everyone is innocent until proven guilty in a court of law, even when they're found lying in bed naked on top of a four-year-old girl. She choked down her anger and headed out to the ambulance bay to help 52's crew unload their patient.

Claire joined the second team of nurses, doctors, techs and security guards who swarmed the back doors of the rig before it even came to a full a stop. She, Jim and six other strong hands stepped forward and grabbed hold of the overloaded stretcher as the paramedic on board, Kia Rydell, rolled the patient out of the ambulance.

"Forty-two year old male patient presenting with multiple blunt force trauma injuries..." Kia reported as the stretcher's wheels hit the ground and this new group banged through the E.D. doors. Claire didn't bother following them into the treatment room; she headed back to her paperwork.

She had almost managed to finish up her run form when a muffled howling sound dragged her attention to the front of the Emergency Department. Sarge and two other uniforms were towing Bethie's mother in through the same sliding glass doors her daughter and boyfriend had just been rushed through. She was barefoot, handcuffed and still covered in blood, only now it was drying, causing her hair to stick out in clumps.

"BETTTTTHHHIIIIIEEEEE! BETTTTTTHHHIEEEEE, I'm so SORRRRRRRYYYYYY! BETTTTTHHHIIEEE, I want my daughter! Please take me to my daughter!"

The cops wrestled the distraught woman into one of the smallish rooms used for psych patients and got her pinned down in four point restraints. A nurse administered a quick injection of vitamin H that cut the keening to a drugged mumbling, and peace was once more restored to the Pine Hills Hospital Emergency Department.

"Shit, that was intense," Sarge said, flopping down in the chair next to Claire.

"What's the matter, 90 lb. hysterical mothers who almost lost their daughters to pedophilic cocksuckers a little too much for Albany's finest?"

"Hey, you know what they say about people that get all fired up on adrenalin...she had the strength of ten hookers flying the PCP express."

"Sorry I must have missed that angel dusted hooker to distraught mother conversion table in my EMS manual."

"Well look it up next time. How's the kid?"

"Alive. Not much more, but they're working on her. Any idea what really happened?"

"Everything's still preliminary but the Mom's story is holding up so far. Co-worker came in early for her and she went straight home after leaving her lunch in the store restroom. We've preliminarily identified the blood bag as one George Calvin. And get this: the guy was a professor at NYCC, head of the English Literature department. Want to know how we I.D'd him so quick?"

"I don't know...his live-in girl friend tell you?"

"Nah, *lots* more fun that that."

"All right, go ahead since you seem so hot to tell it..."

"Well, I thought you of all people would appreciate this. It seems the good professor is quite the poet. Last year, he even won an award for his prodigious talent, a beautiful crystal obelisk from the Academic Poetry Society of America."

"Let me guess, the trophy was the 'first thing Bethie's mother picked up', right?"

"Bingo. We counted at least 20 stab wounds on his sunny side up side alone. I'm sure the docs will find a few more when they clean him up."

"Wow, she really went Momma-Bear all over his ass."

"Yeah, and that takes us to where she stashed the assault weapon."

"No...you mean?"

"Yep. We thought it was some kind of sex toy at first, but those APSA folks are pretty classy. They engrave the recipient's name, their name, the date. and what the award is for right on the bottom. Saved us a butt load of time, if you'll pardon the pun."

It really wasn't all that hilarious, but the image struck Claire's morbid funny bone and she and Sarge got the giggles. They struggled to keep it under control, given the circumstances; but the more they tried to swallow the laughter, the more carried away they got. It took a series of dirty looks from the nurses and a pen barrel jammed into her thigh to finally dry up Claire's cackle attack.

"Well, I'm glad you two are having a good time," head E.D. nurse Karen Morgan said, slamming the chart down on the counter in front of them.

"Sorry Karen, it was one of those traumatic laugh-or-go-insane moments, I guess."

"Yes, Nurse Morgan, my apologies," Sarge choked out. "Now can you tell us how the patient is doing?"

Karen looked back and forth between the paramedic and the cop and decided they'd been chastised enough. She dropped the frosty, professional tone and filled them in on what the doctors had been able to do...and not do. The girl would live, but they wouldn't know if she would regain consciousness for days, maybe weeks.

"Was she sexually assaulted?" Sarge asked.

"Yes. There are multiple vaginal and anal tears and lacerations: some new, some partially healed, some scarred over. Unfortunately, it looks like the abuse had been going on for quite awhile."

"Any signs of abuse other than sexual?"

"No. No old breaks, signs of cuts or burn marks, or any of the usual trauma we normally see. She also doesn't have any record of E.D. visits, either here or at other area hospitals."

"That doesn't mean there wasn't abuse, though," Claire said quietly, staring at the pen she was twiddling between her fingers. "Sometimes the worst kinds of beatings are the ones that don't leave any physical marks."

"Huh?" Sarge said.

"She means verbal, Sarge. You know, words hurt, like being cursed at and threatened."

"Not just curses or direct threats. It can be an organized campaign of terror. Constant daily fear, emotional blackmail, mind games. There's a whole menu of non-physiological torture that some sick fucks will serve up if you give them the chance."

Claire raised her eyes to see both Sarge and Karen staring at her like she had just confessed to being an alien from another planet. It was a look she'd seen before, and the reason she generally kept her mouth shut when this type of subject matter came up.

"Karen, any update on Professor Pervert's condition yet?" Claire asked quickly, changing the subject.

"He's critical but stable, don't ask me how or why. Over two dozen stab wounds, a fractured skull and other assorted head trauma, liters of blood loss, not to mention the intestinal and rectal damage. It's a freaking miracle he even survived the ride in here, no criticism meant toward the crew that brought him in."

"So what are his chances?" Sarge asked.

"They're taking him up to surgery right now. If he makes it off the table, I'd say he's got maybe a 50/50 chance of walking out of here."

"And Bethie's chances?" Claire asked.

Karen dropped her eyes and fussed with the stethoscope looped around her neck. "Claire, you've been at this long enough to know none of this is written in stone. We're all just taking our best guesses with the information we have. Kids are stronger and more resilient than we give them credit for. There's always a chance she'll wake up and start yelling her head off for ice cream."

"Or for her mother," Claire said. "What is the story on the Mom, Sarge?" Karen asked.

"We just brought her in. She's resting comfortably in Room 12, four pointed and basking in the glow of a Haldol cocktail."

"Terrific. Is there a next of kin or someone that we can get to sign the consent forms and fill out the paperwork?"

"The guys are tracking down family members now. As soon as we find someone, we'll get them down here."

"What's going to happen to Bethie's Mom?" Claire asked Sarge.

"We'll get her cleaned up and medically checked and cleared while she's here. Then we'll take her back to the precinct, where she'll be charged with assault to start. If he dies, they'll upgrade it to homicide."

JAN KOZLOWSKI

"But she only attacked him to save her daughter..."

"C'mon Claire you're no newbie. You know how this stuff works. The guy's in critical condition, and she confessed to working him over. It's our job to bring her in. Whether she gets arrested for first or second degree assault, attempted murder or manslaughter, that's all up to the lawyers and the courts."

"I know. I *know*. But it pisses me off all the same. Here's a woman who found out what her...man...was doing, and she stopped him. She should get a fucking medal, not spend the rest of her life in prison."

"I understand where you're coming from, Claire," Sarge said. "But she could have called the cops *before* aerating him. She could have called social services. Shit, she could have left his ass. But she didn't. She chose violence. She chose to break the law, so now she has to pay the price."

"Sarge, you saw those wounds. Do you honestly think those were the results of a conscious, sane *decision* on her part? She came home and here's this bastard on top of her little girl. Do you think you would have done any better in that situation? What if that had been Debbie? She's, what, seventeen now...but what if, back when she was four..."

"I would have double-tapped the son of a bitch. Put one in his balls and one in his brain, and then gone after my ex for allowing a repulsive piece of protoplasm anywhere near my baby. After that, I probably would have turned it into a hat trick and eaten my gun, just so I wouldn't have to live through the resulting bullshit."

"See?"

"See nothing. I'm speaking for myself as a father, not as a member of law enforcement. I understand what she was feeling, and I hear you, too. But the law's the law. Sometimes it's not right, and it's not fair, but it's the best we've got," Sarge said.

"Some best when she's probably going to end up serving more time for assaulting that piece of shit than he would have gotten for abusing Bethie. And, you know that after he does his slap-on-the- wrist time, probably as part of some sort of cushy "offender" program, he's going to be right back out there while Bethie's mother rots away down at Bedford Hills."

"Like I said, it's not completely fair, but what you gonna do?" Sarge said, hoisting himself to his feet.

There has to be something, Claire thought as she put the finishing touches on her report.

"Hey, there you are," Jim said leaning in over the counter and grabbing a lollipop from the bowl on the desk. "I just got a call from company Dispatch, they want us back available to APD ASAP."

"Yeah, yeah, tell them to L-M-N-O-P me."

CHAPTER FOUR

"Paramedic car 45 clearing Albany Memorial."

"10-4, 45."

As soon as Claire hung up the mike, her cell rang. "Shit, it's Company Dispatch," she said, punching the talk button a little harder than necessary.

"Claire, it's Eileen. Don't stress, I'm not going to chew your ass for sitting at the hospital. A phone call came in for you. I'm sorry to have to tell you this, but your father is in the hospital."

Claire felt her stomach drop. "My father?"

"Yeah. The caller was a woman named Olivia Herschel, but she said you would know her as Olivia O'Neil. Evidently, you went to high school together. She said your father had some sort of an accident and he's at Paxton General hospital. You can get in touch with her at 860-555-7933."

"7933. Got it. Thanks, Eileen."

"Sure, hope everything's okay. It's tough when they get older, isn't it?"

"Yeah, it is. Thanks."

"Everything okay?" Jim asked as she snapped her phone shut. "You look like you're about to code on me."

"Yeah, no...it's just...nothing."

"Hey look, I might just be your clueless partner, but even I can tell whatever that was, it sure as hell wasn't 'nothing'. Your father okay?"

"I don't know. There was an accident and he's in the hospital. At least that was the message."

"So call and find out. You wrote the number on your hand."

Claire stared at her hand like she didn't recognize it and that it might, in fact, be dangerous. "Maybe after shift. You know how they feel about personal calls on company time."

"Claire, your father's in the hospital. I think this qualifies as an emergency. Let me call Dispatch and have them take us offline for a few minutes. I'll go grab something to eat and you can have some privacy."

Claire could feel her lizard brain, her survivor's brain, whispering to her. *Normal people would say thank you and make the phone call. If you don't, they'll think something's wrong with you and ask a lot of questions.*

"Okay, Jim. Thanks. And I'm sorry. I guess the news shook me up more than I thought."

"No problem, family stuff will do that to you."

Family stuff. Jim called them in on a 10-7, car temporarily out of service, pulled the ambulance into the nearest fast food joint and wandered off in search of something resembling lunch. Claire sat staring at the number scrawled on her hand in blue ink. Family stuff. *Call or they'll wonder why.* The Lizard Brain again. *Appear normal at all costs, remember?*

Claire took a deep breath, snapped open her phone and dialed. She didn't know if she was hoping for a live person or voice mail to answer.

"Claire, I'm so glad you got back to me! I'm only sorry it's under these circumstances."

Damn, it was human Olivia. And she sounded impossibly perky, too. And damn caller ID: she'd never get used to people already knowing who she was.

"Hi, Olivia...it's been a long time. About Dad..." *Is "Dad" right? What do normal people call their fathers? Daddy? Father? No, Dad is fine. Dad is neutral.* "Can you tell me what happened?"

"The volunteer ambulance brought him into the Paxton General emergency room this morning. Paul Isaacs, the kid that helps him out around The Fish Camp, found him at the bottom of his front steps and called 911. Looks like he's got a broken right leg, a strained right wrist and a bruised hip. He's actually really lucky, especially with those stairs being so steep...well, I'm sure I don't have to remind you..."

"Nope, you sure don't." *Insert fake laugh here*, Claire's lizard instructed. "How bad was the break?"

"Again, he was lucky. Dr. Thompson said it was a clean tib/ fib fracture. He put him in a full leg cast and if he behaves himself, he'll get it off in eight weeks or so."

"Well, that's good news then. Glad to hear he'll be okay. Thanks so much for letting me know. It's been great talking to you, but I really have to get back to..."

"No, Claire, wait...I think it would be a good idea if you came back home to see him."

"Did he ask for me? Did he ask you to call me?"

"To be honest, no, he didn't."

"So what's this all about then, Olivia? We were good friends in high school. You know, probably more than anyone else, what it was like living with that bastard. You knew what he was like, some of it anyway. What in the hell makes you think I have any interest in laying eyes on him ever again?"

"I'm sorry Claire. I know this is coming out of nowhere and bringing up a lot of stuff you'd rather forget, but please. Just listen to me for a minute, really hear me...remember how we used to talk about our dreams and goals our senior year?"

"Yes, but I don't see what that has to do with..."

"Just think back. Remember when we used to walk the old dam? I've never forgotten those conversations. In fact, they were a big part of the reason I became a social worker here in town. That's also how I found out about your Dad's accident. Thankfully, it's hospital policy to call in Social Services anytime a patient is admitted with no next of kin or emergency contacts."

Olivia had always been chatty, but Claire felt like she was being battered by a verbal tidal wave. Torrents of words were crashing over her, only one or two making any kind of sense before tumbling off downstream. The headache that had begun with the words "your father is in the hospital" pulsed behind her eyes. She sighed and switched the phone to her other ear. She doubted Olivia had even taken a breath.

"...and then when I found out it was him, and heard that he was being admitted for at least three days plus maybe a week to ten days at the rehab facility, I knew I had to find you and try to convince you to come back home and do the right thing. So I looked you up on Google and found the news story about how you saved that family from the gas leak. I couldn't find a home or cell phone number for you, but the name of your ambulance company was right there, so I called them up instead and left you the message. I'm so glad you returned my call, and so fast, too."

"Olivia," she interrupted, trying to cap off the word geyser. "What do you mean, the right thing?"

"You know, the right thing, just like we used to talk about all the time, especially when we were out at the dam."

Light was slowly beginning to dawn in the recesses of Claire's muddled mind. "Impossible. I couldn't. My job...and I have a life here now."

"You don't have to stay forever. Depending how long he's in the hospital and how long it takes to clean the place out and get it fixed up for him, you could be back to your life in a couple of weeks. And you'd sleep soundly knowing that you had stepped up and taken care of an important piece of family business."

"Olivia...I...I don't know."

"Look, why don't you at least drive down for the day. It's what, two and a half, three hours or so. We'll sit and talk somewhere quiet, have a cup of coffee, or something stronger if you'd like, and talk. Afterwards, if you're still dead set against it, you can turn around and go straight back to Albany, no harm, no foul. And I promise I'll never bring the subject up again."

Claire paused, her head pounding. "Okay," she answered slowly. "Yeah, maybe I'm nuts, but okay. This is my last shift on this rotation. I have three days off starting at 7pm tonight. I'll tell them I'm heading down to Connecticut to check on my father and I'll let them know if I'm going to need more time off after I find out what his situation is."

"Fair enough. Meet me at Lenny's, 10am-ish?"

"Don't tell me the old guy is still in business?"

Olivia laughed. "Not only is he still open, the restaurant made Nutmegger Magazine's Hidden Restaurant Gems List last month."

"You've got to be kidding me. That must have pissed him off."

"Like you won't believe. Don't worry, he'll tell you all about it. See you tomorrow then?"

"10am."

Claire closed her phone and slumped back in the seat.

"The old man okay?" Jim asked, climbing back into the ambulance with his greasy bags of food-like substances.

"Sounds that way, but I'll find out in person tomorrow."

"Good. I won't worry about you so much if I know you're going home to spend some time with your family."

CHAPTER FIVE

The clock in her ancient LeBaron convertible read 9:46 as Claire pulled off Rte. 10 and into Lenny's gravel driveway. Glad to see some things don't change, she thought as she negotiated the pothole strewn parking lot and stopped in front of the ramshackle, run down building. Lenny never had been one to give a shit about appearances. Keeps out the riff raff, he always said.

She shut off the engine and leaned back in the seat. Sleep had been impossible last night, her mind spinning off in a hundred different directions, none of them comforting. Images and sound bites of Bethie and Donovan, as well as memories she thought had banished decades ago flickered, popped and stuttered across her mental screen like a bad movie festival. Eyes open, eyes closed, it didn't matter.

And when the video marathon finally took the odd break, the phantom physical manifestations would creep in, just for a change of pace. So much for her self-awarded I've-Gotten-Over-It badge from Tough Girl U.

You don't have to do this, the lizard whispered in her head. *You don't have to put yourself through all of this. Start the car back up and get the hell out of here. When Olivia calls, tell her you changed your mind. Wish her luck. Tell her you'll do what you can to help long distance. But coming back...dealing with him again, going back to that place, even for a few days or hours is asking too much.* She had escaped once, but every molecule of survival instinct was roaring at her that she wouldn't be so lucky this time.

It had taken her a few minutes yesterday to process what Olivia was talking about when she mentioned their conversations out at the old dam, and the phrase, "the right thing to do". Thirty years ago, the dam had been their safe spot, one of the few places on the camp property where they weren't afraid of being overheard or spied on. That was where Claire had screwed up the courage to tell Olivia some of the things her father had done to her. Olivia had hugged her hard, and then confessed that Claire's father had done things to her as well.

They had cycled through all the stages of grief together that summer, but what had given them the most peace was their shared fantasy of someday making Claire's father pay for what he had done to them, and probably to countless others. They had called it "the right thing" and spent hours concocting elaborate, secret revenge plans, almost all of which ended in the gory, yet humiliating "accidental" death of Benjamin R. Valentin.

Was it possible that Olivia was seriously considering acting out those teenage daydreams? Nah. No way. Middle-aged women, a social worker and a paramedic none the less, did not get together over Lenny's famous griddle cakes to debate the merits of tying a man by his cock to the back of a motor boat to see if he could water ski.

Still, it might just be the exhaustion talking, but she had to admit they were the most entertaining thoughts she'd had running around her head in the past twenty hours or so. She was still smiling as she got out of the car and headed into the restaurant.

* * * *

Claire wondered if she would be able to remember what Olivia looked like. It wasn't like they had agreed to wear cheesy corsages or feather boas or anything else to identify themselves. Of course, just choosing Lenny's as a meeting place cut down on possible crowd issues. Lenny didn't care much for crowds. He also didn't give a damn about money.

The first thing you saw coming through the restaurant door was Lenny's Service Policy posted in big block letters behind the cash register. WE PROUDLY RETAIN THE RIGHT TO REFUSE SERVICE TO ANYONE. If you don't like it, he always said, pointing to the sign, don't let the door hit you in the ass on your way out. And Lenny was serious about it. He considered this restaurant his home and if he didn't like you, or the looks of you, you were gone. And that included several prominent members of the Town Council, all of the Planning and Zoning Board, the publisher of the local newspaper, more than a few of the Paxton police force, and anyone Lenny deemed a poseur or country club scum.

If Lenny's had been an average food joint, no one would have given a shit about one crazy old man banning them from his dumpy restaurant. But the truth was Nutmegger Magazine was, for once, right on the money. Lenny was a culinary genius. Of course, if you actually *called* him that, you'd find your ass laid out in the parking lot, but that didn't change the fact that the man could cook.

"Just born with the knack for it," he used to say when he was in the mood to answer questions. "Some people are wired to fix cars or write books, but for me, it's always been cooking. Been doing it since I could stir a pot in Momma's kitchen. Ain't no trick to it. Do anything for fifty-plus years and you're bound to get it right a fair amount of the time."

Looking back, Claire realized his ongoing war with the town's movers and shakers was probably why she and Olivia had gravitated to Lenny's in the first place. Like the dam, it had felt safe. Not to mention that, for unknown reasons, Lenny had taken a liking to both girls, even offering them the chance to make a little money clearing tables and helping out in the kitchen when he was short-handed.

As she scanned the booths and stools, looking for some sign of Olivia, she wondered how much Lenny had known back then. She knew he had never had any use for her father, but they had never talked about why.

"Hey, Girl! Over here!"

The voice was unmistakable, and when Claire turned, the years fell away like the leaves on an overcooked artichoke. It was Olivia, the best friend she had buried along with all the other memories of this place in order to stay sane. A few more lines, a few more pounds, and a lot more grey shot through her brown curls, but Olivia all the same.

"Olivia!" Claire wasn't a hugger or a crier, but by the time

Lenny came out of the back to pry them apart and then get his own hugs in, everyone was a limp, soggy mess.

"C'mon, girls. Olivia said you wanted to talk privately, so I set you up a spot in the back where no one will bother you." Trotting to keep up with the whirl of cook's whites, they followed Lenny back through the kitchen and out the rear door to a large patio area completely enclosed by an eight-foot tall stockade fence.

"What, no barbed wire and guard towers, Len?" Olivia asked, smiling.

"No, smart ass. Guards cost money, but the wire's on back order. Damn Home Warehouse place, they look at you like you've got two heads when you ask for something as simple as a couple of rolls of razor coil. Never had that problem at old Dokey's Hardware. Now, that man knew how to run a business."

The girls waited until Lenny had gone back inside, still muttering about the failure of modern retail establishments, before exploding into giggles.

"It's a shame when people start to mellow, isn't it?" Olivia asked.

"Yep...damn...shame," Claire spit out before another laughing fit took hold. Eventually they calmed down enough to take seats in the metal folding chairs Lenny had put out for them and pour themselves a cup of coffee from the carafe that sat on the giant wooden spool table.

"Thanks for the elegant homecoming party." Claire said, raising her paper cup.

"No problem, girlfriend. All the comfort home can provide. I do have it on good authority, though, that if you hang around long enough, Lenny may be bribed into cooking up some chocolate chip griddle cakes and slab bacon for you."

"Shit, you don't play fair."

"Nope, not since I learned playing fair is a sucker's game."

Silence fell between them as the two women regarded each other across the table. Both realized they had reached a metaphorical cliff and needed to decide whether they should write this off as a pleasant little reunion...or take the jump.

Claire took a deep breath. "Okay, you got me here. Now what?"

"Now we talk."

"About doing the right thing and unfinished family business and other hallucinations of truth, justice and the American way?"

"Maybe, but how about we start with the update on your Dad's condition?"

"It's your party," Claire shrugged, trying to seem blasé, but she couldn't control the tightening of her jaw and the curling of her fingers.

"I talked to the head of his care team this morning. Huge shock, she reported that he's not being particularly cooperative. His orthopedist would like to insert a rod in the leg, but right now he's refusing the surgery. They're still talking at him, though."

"Good luck with that." Claire muttered.

"Well, it would be good luck for us if they're able to talk him into the rod. Surgery would tie him up for at least three days in the hospital and three weeks in a rehab facility."

"Why, are we betting on medical malpractice or institutional incompetence to take him out for us?"

"That would be handy. But no, I had something a little more proactive in mind. As you know, one of the biggest problems in getting a conviction in any type of abuse case is finding evidence that will stand up in court. With him off the property for that long, it would give us the perfect opportunity to go through the whole place and find everything we need to put him away for the rest of his life."

"Everything like what?"

"Photos, souvenirs, videos, toys and equipment with DNA and trace evidence on it. And that's not counting any computer evidence we might find."

"You honestly think he's stupid enough to keep that stuff around the property?"

"Yeah, I do. He's a serial child rapist and he's been getting away with it for decades. Every official in town, and most of the ones in the state go fishing, rent summer cabins or party at the Fish Camp. He thinks he's invincible."

"True, low self-esteem has never been a problem for dear old Dad. And okay, maybe I can buy that there's incriminating stuff just laying around somewhere. But my memory of the legal system is that they frown on evidence collected as the result of breaking and entering. Something about fruit of a poisonous tree, if I'm remembering my *Law & Order* episodes correctly."

"Well, that's where you, as legal heir, next of kin and dutiful daughter come in." Olivia paused and watched as Claire's mind played out the connections.

"No."

"Hear me out."

"No. This talk is over." Claire rose from her chair and made for the restaurant's back door.

CHAPTER SIX

"Done so soon?" Lenny called out as Claire banged into the kitchen.

"Done. Yeah, that describes it. I'm done and I'm out of here. No offense, it was great seeing you again, and if I never said thanks for all you did for me when I was a kid, I'm saying it now. You probably saved my life and I appreciate it."

"If you *really* appreciated it, girly-girl, you'd sashay your ass back outside and give your friend's plan some serious consideration instead of running off... again."

Claire swung around and glared at the old man. How dare he... and then, staring into his steely blue eyes, she realized he was right. And more than that, as tough as he acted, he had cared about her, and she had hurt him when she left town without even saying goodbye. She had been so young and scared, running to save her own life, but she had never even considered the people she had left behind -Lenny and Olivia.

Her shoulders slumped as the flight and fight drained out of her. "You're right, Lenny."

"Usually am, and it'd do you well to remember it. Now go let your friend finish saying her piece, and I'll be along directly with something to throw down your throats."

Olivia was helping herself to another cup of coffee when Claire rejoined her on the patio.

"Pretty sure that the old man would stop me, huh?"

"I figured either he would, or you'd stop yourself."

Claire shook her head in defeat and slid back into her seat. "Please tell me this isn't going where I think it's going."

"You always had a knack for being a jump or two ahead of

everyone else. Don't shoot me for saying this, but you're just like your father in that respect."

"Insult me all you like. Just don't sit there and tell me you expect me to walk into that hospital and volunteer to play nurse maid to that bastard."

"It's the only chance we have of conducting a legal search, one that has even a possibility of holding up in court."

"There's got to be another way. Get a private investigator. Send someone in under cover as a camper or health inspector... anything. Look, if it's a matter of money, I've got a little saved that I can..."

"Tried it. Tried it. And, oh yeah, tried it, along with about twelve dozen other even more, creative let's say, gambits. None of them made it past the driveway. What do you think I've been doing down here for the past twenty years, playing hopscotch?"

"No, but..."

"There are no 'buts' left. Believe me, I've looked. And just to add to the fun and excitement, this announcement went up on The Fish Camp website last week." Olivia dug a piece of paper out of her pocket, unfolded it and handed it across the table.

"Shit." The banner across the top of the print out read: Valentin's Fish Camp Welcomes the Tiny Miss Western Hemisphere Pageant's Summer Bootcamp!

"Shit."

"You already said that," Olivia pointed out. "It bears repeating...and I'm still trying to process here. I guess, in my head, I convinced myself that he had just fucked you and me up, and that was it. Damn it, I should have known better. God knows I see it every day on the job. I know there're never just one or two victims. Even if they get caught and go to jail, even if an irate citizen castrates them with a rusty cat food can lid, they'll still find a way to get their rocks off."

"Cut yourself some slack. Remember, I wasn't much faster at figuring this out than you were. My theory is that part of it is wishful thinking and part of it is self-protection. You don't want to think about what happened, and you certainly don't want to think that it happened or is happening to anyone else. Because that makes it even more horrible."

"But he *did* do it to others, didn't he?"

"Yeah, he did. Lots of others."

"You know for sure?"

"Over the past fifteen years, I tracked down 42 women who confessed to me that he had molested them. There were another nineteen who wouldn't or couldn't say the words, and about a hundred more who either wouldn't talk to me when they found out what I wanted, or who had either died or disappeared."

"61 women?"

"At the minimum. Probably double that number...or more."

"All those victims, over all those years, and no one has ever gone to the cops?"

"Did you? Did I?"

"But there must have been women who were...braver?"

"Or dumber? Or less concerned about the possible consequences?"

Claire nodded.

"Yes, I have a reliable source that said there were women who went to the cops. But no charges were ever filed, no formal complaints were ever recorded, and no official reports were ever even taken."

"I always knew he had friends in the police department. Hell, half the force was usually out on the lake fishing, and Chief what's- his-name spent more time hanging out at the Lodge than he probably spent in his office."

"No question the town cops had your father's back, and I'm not giving them any kind of a pass, but you've got to admit that the stories any of us have to report are pretty sick, twisted, and frankly not high on the believability scale. It's hard enough for people to accept that someone they think they know so well is capable of sexually assaulting a child, much less serially assaulting multiple children over a span of decades. Add a particularly nasty kink factor to it, and you can't exactly blame them for throwing up a denial wall."

"And the pervert wins."

"Until now...if you'll help." Claire looked down at the paper she still held in her hand.

"You're positive he's still active?" "Do *you* think it's a happy coincidence that come July there will be fifty little beauty pageant hopefuls under the age of twelve running around a place called The Fish Camp?"

"No... no, it's abso-fucking-lutely *not* a coincidence. But how does this even happen? How does he even have a fucking website, let alone the juice and the contacts to make something like this happen?"

"He has help. A couple of months ago, he started working with a public relations pro who set him up with a website, social networks, the whole nine yards. Thanks to her, the Fish Camp is now being promoted as a fun, kitschy kind of retro place with all the amenities of the 21st century."

"Who in their right mind would...?"

"My baby sister, Tandy. Would and did."

CHAPTER SEVEN

"I thought Tandy was living large and happily ever after somewhere near Atlantic City?"

"She was, but you know the story...what looks like forever at age 19 looks like a prison sentence at 33. She and David had themselves a nasty divorce. He got the PR firm, she got the cash and came back here to lick her wounds and start over."

"Start over, sure. But with The Fish Camp?"

"I would never admit this to anyone but you, but as vomit-inducing as it sounds, I think she always had a thing for your father."

"Is Tandy one of the 61?"

"No. I tried to bring up the subject a few years ago, but she had a nuclear meltdown about how dare I slander such a wonderful man, and if she ever heard me spreading lies like that again, she would personally hire the best defamation lawyer on the East Coast and make sure he sued the crap out of me on your father's behalf."

"Nice."

"Yeah, but consistent. Even when she was a kid, she used to follow him around. I warned her a million times, tried to tell her that whatever she did, don't be alone with him, but she wouldn't listen. Even when she got too old for him, she still spent the summers tagging around after him anyway."

"I don't remember that."

"You were gone by then. Remember, Tandy's five years younger than us. You jetted out of here just before your 18th birthday."

Silence fell between the two women. Olivia busied herself pouring both of them more coffee.

"Olivia, I'm sorry."

"Sorry for what happened with Tandy, or for taking off?"

"For both. For everything. For leaving, for Tandy, for not saying goodbye...and for not being able to separate our friendship from all the bad shit I tried to leave behind."

Olivia leaned across the table and took Claire's hands in hers. "It took me years to understand, and to stop being mad at you. It wasn't until I started searching out other ex-campers and talking to them that I realized why you left like that. He threatened to kill you, didn't he?"

"Yes."

"And you believed him?"

"You would have, too, if the son of a bitch had taken you out to the swamp and shown you his body part collection."

Olivia took a deep breath and squeezed Claire's hands so hard she thought the bones would crack.

"The swamp," Olivia repeated, a cold, humorless smile flickering across her face. "That brilliant bastard."

"You knew about the bodies?"

"Not for sure, but I figured he must have had a plan to get rid of anyone he couldn't intimidate, terrify or otherwise completely control. Not to mention that there were a few too many people I tried to contact that seemed to have disappeared off the face of the earth. I always assumed he buried them in the woods, but dumping the bodies in the swamp would cut his work in half, with even less chance that anyone would stumble over any remains accidently."

"God knows I never would have. I was scared to death of that place, and he knew it. The day I left, he came up behind me while I getting into my car in the Lodge parking lot. He grabbed my wrist, dragged me out of the car and told me to come with him like a good girl or he'd break my arm like a chicken wing.

"He led me out to the swamp, right down to that old bateau bridge. He pushed me out to the middle pontoon and made me stand there while he pulled this big fishing chain up out of the wa- ter. At first I didn't see anything but metal links, but then these... pieces started coming up. Body pieces. Some were just bones, some were rotting and half eaten with shreds of clothing hanging off of them. And some looked...fresh."

"Oh, God."

"I was sure that was it. He was going to kill me, cut me up and hang me on that chain for the swamp creatures to snack on. But then he started to laugh. That's when I finally *got* what he was really about. He absolutely could have gotten away with killing me right then and there, but what long-term enjoyment would that have given him? Sure, he would have gotten a charge out of it for the time it took him to dispose of me. But what he was really getting off on was how terrified I was. He loved that I was pissing my pants and choking back vomit. He even had a hard-on. I could see it.

"He dropped the chain back in, grabbed me by my hair, and forced my face down over the edge until I was about an inch above where the line disappeared into the water. Then he whispered in my ear, 'Happy 18th birthday, baby. I know it's a little early, but I wanted to give you a little preview of what I had planned for your big day. Then he started laughing again and let me go.

"I bolted out of there so fast I left one of my sneakers behind, somewhere in the muck. I made it back to the car, found my keys and got the fuck out of there. I automatically headed for Lenny's but then I started thinking that's exactly where he would expect me to go. Either there or to your house. So I just kept driving."

"And that's how you ended up in Albany?"

"Yeah. I grabbed as much money as I could out of the ATM in the center of town and hit the highway. I didn't even stop to get a change of clothes or a pair of shoes until I was at a rest stop on the Mass Pike. By then it was so late no one looked twice at a mess of a girl buying flip flops, Harvard sweats and a six-pack of granny panties. I cleaned up as best I could in the rest room, stuffed my old clothes in the trash barrel, and kept going."

Claire stopped talking and sat there staring off into space, her body present, but her mind lost on a deserted highway, battling twenty-year-old demons in the dead of the night.

"Claire, I'm so sorry." Claire shook her head in protest, but Olivia overrode her. "Not just for what happened then, but for making you dredge it all up again. I didn't know it was that bad. I knew he was...but I never thought he'd...to his own daughter... damn."

Olivia trailed off, dropped Claire's hands and slouched back in the chair. "We can't do this. *You* can't do this. We'll just have to come up with another way or...or...."

"Or forget it completely? Is that what you were going to say?"

Olivia nodded and made a strangled sound, like the words were trying to punch their way out of her throat. "And that means he wins...again. Not only does he get away everything he did to us, and to God knows how many other women and families, but he gets to keep doing it for the rest of his unnatural, disgusting life. Because everyone is afraid of him. Because *I'm* afraid of him. That's what it comes down to, doesn't it?"

Claire wasn't talking to Olivia anymore. There was someone else she needed to convince more. *I can't let him keep doing this. I'm not a kid anymore. I can't let him scare me anymore. What's the worst thing he can do, kill me? He murdered me years ago. He just forgot to add my body to his fishing chain. I can't let the bastard get away with this, not again.*

Olivia's right, this is our best chance, maybe the only chance left. I can do this. I can play nice. I bet he would even get off on that. Claire snapped out of her self-induced semi-trance and refo- cused her eyes on her friend.

"Olivia, that's it. That's the way to play this. You were right. The bastard would eat up the 'dutiful daughter' shit with a spoon. Having me back at the house, taking care of his every need, the situation would be too potentially orgasmic for him to pass up. And even if he doesn't trust me, he'll be willing to risk it for a shot at being able to spend some quality time abusing and torturing me again."

Claire watched as Olivia stared at her across the table, measuring her, before reaching across, taking her hand and saying quietly, "Okay, let's do this."

CHAPTER EIGHT

Three hours, a plate of Lenny's griddle cakes, and several cups of coffee later, Claire marched through the main doors of Paxton General Hospital and headed straight for the Information Desk.

"May I help you?" the pink-smocked, grandfatherly volunteer asked.

"I hope so," Claire said, trying to look properly frazzled and concerned. "I'm looking for my father, Benjamin Valentin. I got a call saying he had an accident yesterday morning and was brought here."

"Yes, I heard something about that," he said, running his finger down a list of names. "Here he is. He's up on the second floor, north wing, Room 228. You'll need to sign in and take a visitor's pass."

While Claire leaned down to fill in her name and the time, she felt the man staring at her and she tried not to freak out. She was back in her hometown, and she was going to have to get used to people recognizing her face or name.

"So you're Val's daughter, all grown up," he said as she clipped the laminated card with the big, plastic V on it to her shirt. "I haven't seen you around the Camp since you were a little bit of a thing."

"I've been living out of state since right after high school."

"Oh well, that happens a lot. All but one of my four went to college out of state and ended up staying put after they graduated. It's a shame, but you kids have got to live your own lives, I suppose. Tell Val that Quinn said to get better quick. Opening Day's coming up fast, and it just wouldn't seem right to kick off fishing season anywhere else but the Camp."

"I'll be sure to tell him. Thanks!"

Claire headed across the lobby to the elevators but changed her mind and banged through the door marked Stairs instead. It was only one flight up to North 2, but she walked slowly and used the time to pull herself together.

She and Olivia had decided that the best way to go was to keep their story as simple and straightforward as possible. Claire would say that she'd heard through an old friend that her father had had an accident and was in the hospital. Even though they had been estranged for a long time, the news had still hit her pretty hard. After a sleepless night, she had decided to come down on her day off to see for herself how he was doing, and maybe try to mend some fences before it was too late.

Olivia's theory was that most everyone could identify and sympathize with a difficult parent/child relationship and the guilt, ambivalence and craziness it caused. So once Claire showed up and made it clear she was there to try to help, the professionals would more than likely back off and give her and her father the space to work it out for themselves. Then it would just be a matter of dealing with her father, and playing up to whichever one of his sick fantasies would get her back inside The Camp property.

It was a good plan. And now – as she finally discovered the hidden alcove where Room 228 was located and faced the closed, windowless door – she knew the only thing she wasn't sure about was if she had the guts to pull it off or not.

Claire raised her fist to knock, but found herself jumping for her life as the door whooshed inward and a blue scrub suit barreled out, followed closely by a spinning metal UFO and a stream of curses. She flattened herself against the wall as the food dish caught up to the scrub suit, and both tumbled into a parked, canvas-sided laundry cart.

"And don't come back with anymore of that shit on a shingle. For what I'm paying, you'd think you were flying Cordon fucking Bleu meals in on the Concorde. So goddammit, bring me something edible."

Keeping a wary eye out for more airborne appetizers, Claire ran over to check on the condition of the hapless nurse's aide. "Are you okay?" she asked, as he swiped his eyes free of whatever gunk they were serving today.

"Yeah, I think so. Damn, that is one mean son of a bitch."

"No argument here. Let me help you up."

The young man took her hand and levered himself out of the tangle of dirty linens and half-collapsed bin. Once he was on his feet, Claire couldn't help notice how good he looked, even covered in the remains of her father's meal. Tall and dark haired, with what looked like a lean, rock climber's body hiding under his scrubs, he was exactly the kind of guy that had always gotten her motor going.

"Thanks," he said, unleashing a killer smile to go with the rest of the package.

"As the daughter of the aforementioned son of a bitch, it's the least I can do."

"Oh man, I'm sorry. That was really unprofessional. No disrespect intended..."

"Given the circumstances, I'm impressed by your restraint. I don't know if I would have been that charitable. And besides, I'm the one that should be apologizing: not only for what he just did, but probably for a whole bunch of stuff you haven't told me about yet."

"Yep, he's certainly been keeping all of North 2 on our toes since he landed here..." His cognac brown eyes flicked up to the analog clock hanging in the hallway. "...25 hours, 14 minutes and 8 seconds ago."

"Sorry. Again. I'm Claire, by the way. Claire Valentin. I just got in from Albany."

"Nice to meet you, Claire. I'm Zack McCauley, your father's nurse. I'd shake your hand, but our cafeteria food is toxic when applied topically."

"A floor nurse with a sense of humor? I'll admit that's a nice change from what I'm used to but, for some reason I was under the impression that you were a CNA."

"Understandable mistake. You see a medical professional covered in unsavory substances, and naturally you think certified nurse's aide."

"Or Emergency Medical Technician..."

"Or EMT, but unfortunately this particular patient has managed to scare off all the aides and most of the other nurses, several doctors, the X-ray department, and the entire housekeeping staff. The only ones who have been able to handle him so far are Harriet down in Admissions, who cage fights on weekends, and Big Tommy, the Paxton volunteer EMT who single-handedly strapped him to a backboard and shoved him into the back of the ambulance in the first place."

"Wow, it sounds like I owe both of them a show of appreciation. Do you think a steak dinner would cover it?"

"I don't know about Big Tommy, but my guess is Harriet prefers her meat raw...and probably still twitching," he said with a deep chuckle.

Damn, he even had a great laugh. "And how about you, Nurse McCauley? How can I show you my appreciation?" She didn't realize how blatant the words sounded until they had already left her mouth. What the hell was she doing? She didn't flirt, and certainly not with Joe Hottie, Male Nurse here, who had to be at least ten years her junior.

"All in a day's work, Ma'am," Zack responded, tipping an invisible hat to her.

Good, he's ignoring it, Claire thought. And he called me Ma'am, code word for old lady. Maybe I can still walk out of here with a little dignity intact.

"...but if you really feel the need to thank me for risking life and limb in service to your Pater Familias, how about letting me buy you a non-toxic beverage at this great little place I know called Lenny's?"

"I'm...I'd...Umm," she stuttered.

"No pressure. It was just a..."

Crash.

"God damned motherfucking son of a cunt!"

CHAPTER NINE

Claire and Zack turned in unison and shoved through her father's door.

"Mr. Valentin, are you okay?" Zack called, out running toward the crumpled figure on the floor beside the bed.

"Just peachy, asshole. Get me up!"

"Hold on a minute. Let me make sure you haven't done any more damage to yourself before we start bouncing you around." Zack knelt down and performed a quick body survey, checking his patient's neck, back, hip and cast while Valentin kept up a constant patter of complaints and insults.

"Enjoy that, did you, Nursie?"

"I can honestly say to you, Mr. Valentin, no, I did not. But, everything seems okay, so let's get you back into bed."

"Let me give you a hand," Claire offered, stepping forward.

"Great, get under his left side there, grab my arm behind his back. Good. Now lock your other arm under his hips with me and lift."

"Nursie," Valentin said, squinting up at Zack. "Save your breath, this girl could teach a class on handling patients. This is my daughter, Claire. She's a decorated paramedic up in Albany."

Claire felt her stomach free fall into her sneakers. He knew. He not only recognized her after all these years, he knew where she was and what she did for a living.

"Yep, my girl once saved a whole family from a gas leak. She and her partner dragged five kids and four adults out of their fourth floor apartment before the fire department even showed up. They said another few minutes in that gas or even one little spark from a light switch, and all of them would have died. And not to mention, she sucked down so much gas saving them she ended up in the hospital on oxygen herself."

"Impressive." Zack said as he locked eyes with Claire over her father's head. Claire could feel the blush creeping up her neck and flushing her face. "He exaggerates."

"The hell I do. The city gave her a commendation for bravery. I've got the newspaper article framed and hanging on my living room wall."

"I'd like to hear more about that sometime. Ready to move him?"

"One...two...three." Claire called as they lifted, pivoted and lowered her father back in his bed.

"Smooth," Zack said tucking in the blankets and snapping the bed's safety rail back into place. "Any time you want to leave the mean streets and come to work at a place with indoor plumbing, I can pull a few strings."

"Fuck that noise. If she comes back home, it won't be to wipe asses and clean up puke in this dump."

"Now, Dad." Claire choked out. The word "Dad" sounded odd and foreign to her ears. "Nobody's talking about me coming back, and I'm sure Paxton General is a perfectly fine hospital."

"Then why the fuck was I just taking a sight-seeing tour of the underside of my bed?"

"That's a good question, Mr. Valentin. How did you manage to get out of bed? I distinctly remember the rails being up before you started pelting me with food."

"I thought I heard my little girl's voice out in the hall, and when she didn't come in...I...I wanted to make sure that she didn't leave before I could see her."

"Oh, Dad," Claire's said, trying to keep her mental balance while her mind wobbled and threatened to spin out of control. This whole conversation was becoming weird squared, like The Simpsons' spin on Gabriel Garcia Marquez's novels. Any minute she expected a talking coyote to wander in and start speaking in erudite riddles.

Her father smiled at her, "It's the truth. I don't know what I would've done if you'd left before I got a chance to see you. I wouldn't have blamed you, but...well, I'm just glad you're here."

This man was not acting like the father she had grown up with. The offensive language and reprehensible behavior towards the hospital staff was him all day, but the way he was being with her... this was unfamiliar territory. Never in her whole life could she recall him ever calling her "his little girl" in any but the creepiest of ways, or being glad to see her, not even during the Ward Cleaver, Perfect Dad performances he insisted on playing out whenever they went anywhere as "a family".

She had never bought into the theory that people were capable of permanently changing who they really were, especially as they get older. As a paramedic, she spent a fair amount of time with the elderly, and in her experience, they usually ended up a more concentrated version of whatever they were when they were younger. The nice ones got nicer and the nasty ones seemed convinced that aging gave them license to shit on everyone that crossed their paths.

There was no way in hell her father could have changed... could he? She had spent her entire childhood and truthfully, her entire life, living in mortal terror of him. He had abused her, he had done horrible things to her and Olivia and probably a hundred others. And then there were the body parts in the swamp. She knew what she had seen. It hadn't all been a nightmare. Human beings this evil and perverted did not change. It was impossible. This had to be some kind of scam he was running, either on her directly or for Zack's benefit. Nothing else made sense.

She watched him fidget as Zack tried to take his vitals and re-check his cast and bandages. He looked smaller than she remembered. *Yeah, like your basic scorpion,* her lizard brain whispered.

Claire closed her eyes and took a deep breath. It didn't matter. I didn't matter what he was or wasn't any more. This was a job. It was like being back on duty in Albany. It didn't matter how disgusting, horrifying or dangerous the call was, it was her responsibility to get it done. She had promised Olivia and, as corny as it sounds, in her heart, she had also made a promise to all of his other victims. She had been weak and selfish once, but she wasn't going to cut and run again.

CHAPTER TEN

"I'm glad I'm here, too, Dad. It's been too long."

"Well, it sounds like you two have some catching up to do. If you need me, Mr. Valentin, the call button is looped right there on the bed rail. Ms. Valentin, if you'd like, you can stop by the nurse's station later and give me your contact information...to add to your father's file, in case we need to get in touch with you."

"Thanks, Nurse McCauley, I'll make sure to do that."

Claire felt a little thrill run down her spine as she watched Zack and his muscular, almost edible gluteus saunter out of the room. "I wouldn't get my hopes up, girl. That one's got butt pirate written all over him. You should see how he eager he is to give me a sponge bath every time he walks through that door."

"Dad, he's just doing his job. And he only wants my contact info in case something happens to you. If you don't want them to call me, though..."

"No...no...if it's okay with you, it's okay with me. To tell you the truth, I'm a little surprised it IS okay with you, though. And, like I said before, I wouldn't blame you. I can't believe you're even really here after all that shit I put you through as a kid. I know I wouldn't be if the situation was reversed."

"To be honest, I'm a little shocked to be here myself. But I started thinking about it after I heard you were in the hospital, and I knew I had to at least come down and see how you were doing."

"I'm happy you did. It was killing me that I might never have the chance to tell you how sorry I am for...for everything. I know I can't make it up to you, and I don't expect you to ever forgive me, but I hoped one day I could at least see you again and, face to face, take responsibility for what I did to you. You need to know, you never did anything wrong. You were a great kid, a daughter any father would have been proud of. I was the one who was the monster."

Claire felt her legs go rubbery underneath her. The things that he was saying were words she dreamed of hearing from him all her life. She grabbed the back of the visitor's chair to keep from collapsing onto the floor.

She didn't trust herself to speak. Regardless of whether he was telling the truth or not, in the almost eighteen years she spent with him, he had never once admitted he was wrong or sorry or mistaken about anything. She could feel the tears gathering so she lifted her head and stared up, an old trick she had learned to back the waterworks off. When she had gotten herself under control again, she snuck a look over at her father and she could swear she saw the shine of tears in his eyes, too.

"Why?" she whispered. "I need you to tell me why you did those things to me."

He took a deep breath and a single tear slid down his leathery cheek. "I'll tell you, but its no excuse. I...I grew up pretty hard myself, and I did a lot of drinking and drugging to get by. Just before you were born, I got hooked on crystal meth. I know I don't need to tell you what that is or what happens to the stupid assholes that get addicted to it. I used to cook it up myself out in that rundown old shack down by the swamp. It made me crazy, and it made me so sick that not only did I believe I was a god, I believed that it was my duty to act on every perverted, twisted thought that bounced around my skull."

"The swamp?" Claire repeated, as an involuntarily shudder ran through her body.

Noticing his daughter's reaction, Valentin dropped his eyes and stared at his hands. "Yeah, that's why I wanted to make sure you'd never go poking around down there. But... that last day, I was so out of my head. I never meant for it to go that far. I'll never forget the look on your face. It haunted me. It was the image I kept in front of me the whole time I was detoxing: the terror and hatred on your beautiful face when I showed you with those old Halloween decorations."

"Hallo...Halloween decorations? No. I saw those things. I *smelled* them. They weren't decorations, they were real." Claire's mouth went dry.

"I know you believed they were at the time, but they were just cheap plastic body parts left over from a party we had at the Lodge. I fixed them up, added a few old animal bones and tied them on that chain to scare you. I needed you to be so terrified of me that you'd run away and never come back again. See, I knew I losing control to the meth, and I was afraid of what I'd do to you if you didn't get away."

"So you're saying you made me believe you were a some kind of serial killer, on top of all the perverted stuff, in order to *save me?*"

"Granted it wasn't the smartest plan in the world, but it's the best plan a meth head like me was capable of coming up with at the time. And, it worked. You got away. And you got far enough away so that I couldn't be a threat to you while I was still using. That summer I was so bad off, and I was using so much at I couldn't handle being more than a few minutes away from the shack and my Methandfriendsofmine. But you were safe in Albany. And believe it or not, that mattered to the tiny spark of sanity I had left."

"You knew where I was the whole time?"

Valentin nodded. "I called in a couple of favors from some friends in law enforcement."

"I spent years terrified that you'd find me, that one day you'd show up at my door and...and..."

"I know. And as fucking feeble as it sounds, all I can say is that I'm sorry."

He was sorry. Claire felt like a live electrical wire had been inserted into her brain. Her head was filled with a buzzing sound and she couldn't feel her body. He was sorry. All that fear. All that pain. All that shame for all those years. Her Daddy said he was sorry.

But her father was also a liar, a manipulator and a world class deviant. Wasn't he? Was it because of the drugs? Or was he lying about that, too? Every question turned into a Hydra puzzle, spawning three more questions for every answer.

She had to get a grip. She couldn't afford to look too deeply into this right now, or she'd swan dive into a psychological rabbit hole so dark and twisted that there'd be no digging herself out.

She had to focus. Olivia was counting on her. She had to get her head out of her ass and work the plan. Whether he was sorry or not didn't matter now. Even if he truly was sorry. Even if he truly had been a meth head, and had truly quit, it didn't change what he had done...or what he was still capable of doing.

On the job, at least once a shift, one of her frequent flyers would call for a ride to the hospital and/or a detox facility, vowing that this was it, they were never going to drink or use again. And then the next shift, or the next rotation, there they were, back in her ambulance again. Granted, some did manage to quit for a while, but then, a month or six or even a year later, there they were right back on her stretcher, mouthing the same words and making the same heartfelt vows.

She had promised Olivia that she would find a way to get into the Fish Camp and find the evidence they needed to lock him away so he'd never have the opportunity to hurt another child. Nothing else mattered. If there was one thing being the survivor of childhood abuse had taught her, it was the value of being able to compartmentalize. In order to function-- and some days, in order to simply survive-- the smartest thing to do was to pull a Scarlett O'Hara and "think about it tomorrow, at Tara."

Claire took a deep breath, stepped forward and reached for her father's hand. "It's not feeble, Dad...it's a place to start."

CHAPTER ELEVEN

"Knock, knock," a woman's voice called from the other side of the door.

"Fuck. It sounds like that damn social worker Olive something or other. Tell her to go away, or better yet, tell her I died in a fiery wheelchair accident."

"Dad, it's standard hospital policy for social workers to check in with patients who don't have any family or other types of support systems. They're just looking out for you."

"While making damn sure their own fat asses are covered."

"Mr. Valentin, we really need to talk. May I please come in?"

"Yeah. Yeah. Come." Olivia scurried into the room, but made it a point to stay at least an arm's length away from the bed. "Thank you, Mr. Valentin...oh, I'm sorry I didn't realize you had company."

"It's okay, this is my daughter, Claire. She just got back into town. She's a paramedic up in Albany."

"Pleased to meet you Claire, I'm Olivia Herschel, the social worker assigned to your father's care team."

Claire nodded at her since they weren't close enough to shake hands. She and Olivia agreed that the best way to handle their inevitable meeting was to act like total strangers. Both doubted that her father would remember Olivia or her connection to Claire or the Fish Camp.

"Mr. Valentin, we need to talk about your decision to refuse surgery on your leg."

"All right, but don't take all day about it. Remember, I'm a sick man."

"Well, actually Mr. Valentin, that's the crux of the problem," Olivia said, pulling several papers from the manila folder was carrying. "According to these reports, you're not a sick man. Other than your broken leg and other minor injuries, you're an amazingly healthy man for your age. And as such, your insurance company, the hospital and your care team feel that, unless you're willing to change your mind and follow your orthopedist's recommendations, there's no reason for you to remain here at Paxton General."

"You're throwing him out?" Claire asked, genuinely caught off guard. Olivia had been so sure that he'd be hospitalized for weeks.

"But what about rehab? What about physical therapy?"

"The care team does feel that a rehabilitation facility would be the best place for him, and there are quite a few excellent ones here locally. We took the liberty of contacting a few of them and, in fact, at least two representatives have already attempted to meet with your father, but he made them feel, shall we say, less than welcome."

"Dad?"

"I keep telling you people. I don't want the cock-knocking surgery and I *sure* as hell don't want to go to any fucking *facility*. Facilities are where old people go to die...or where they lock up the crazies. And since I'm not ready to die and you can't prove that I'm crazy, you can take your facility and stick it up your collective cunts."

"Dad! I'm sorry, Ms. Hershel, my father is obviously distraught. There must be other options?"

"I don't want their options, Claire. I want to go home."

"I can sympathize, Mr. Valentin, but from what I understand, you live by yourself in a fairly isolated setting. You won't be able to drive, or even walk without crutches for weeks. How are you going to take care of yourself?"

"I'll throw that neighbor boy Paulie, a couple of bucks and he can stop by a couple of times a day to make sure I'm still kicking."

"But what if something happens in between his visits? What if you fall or get stuck in the bathroom? Or have some kind of medical emergency? No, Mr. Valentin, I can't sign off on that as a discharge plan. It's not safe."

"Dad, I think you should reconsider the surgery. They could go in, stabilize your leg, and then when you do get home after rehab, you'll be a lot more able to manage on your own."

"No. No one's cutting me open. I've lived 78 years without some knife-happy bone jockey slicing me up like a side of beef, and I'm not going to start now."

"What about a visiting nurse?"

"That would be fine for the hours that she'd be there. But, particularly for the first couple of weeks, what if something happens during the middle of the night?"

"I'm sure there must be nurses or companions that do round the clock care..."

"There are, but they're expensive. And frankly, their tolerance for...ah...high maintenance patients isn't as great as those of us who work in the public sector."

Valentin sat bolt upright in the bed and jabbed his finger at Olivia. "I know what your little 'high maintenance' euphemism means, lady. I'm not deaf or stupid."

"She didn't mean anything by that, Dad."

"Yeah, she did. But guess what. No matter what she says or how loud she squawks about not signing off on this, the truth of the matter is-- unless she can prove I'm incompetent-- she has no legal right to keep me here against my will."

No, no, no. Claire could see where this was going, and she wasn't prepared for this. She had been mostly okay with the original plan: come down here and hang around while he was in the hospital and rehab. Visit him, talk him into letting her go out and get the house ready for him. And then once she had the keys, blitz through the property, find whatever there was to find and be back in Albany by the time the cops took custody of him.

Going back to The Fish Camp, back to where she grew up, with him...taking care of him...that was never part of the deal.

CHAPTER TWELVE

"Mr. Valentin, there is one other alternative we haven't explored."

Claire turned toward Olivia and shot her a pleading look. "You said your daughter was a paramedic. It's not optimal, but I wouldn't be completely adverse to releasing you to her, as long as she agreed to take responsibility for your home care."

"I...I couldn't ask her to do that. She's got her job and..."

"I'm sure her employer has a family leave policy. Most medical businesses are well aware of situations like these and make provisions for their employees. Right, Ms. Valentin?"

"Yes...you're right, Ms. Herschel. My company does offer family leave as part of our benefit package, but..."

"I know...it would be difficult to take the time away from your husband and kids..."

"Um...no...I don't have...I mean, I'm single and..." Claire could feel the panic setting in. She knew that Olivia was fixated on getting her inside the Camp, and that's why she must be pushing like that. But this couldn't happen. "Ms. Hershel, if I could have a word with you out in the hall..."

"Claire, you don't have to do that. You can say what you have to say in front of me. In fact, I'll say it myself. Ms. Hershel, I was a fuck-up as a father. My daughter left home, with good reasons, twenty years ago, and we haven't seen or talked to each other until she walked through that door a half hour ago. It's not fair or right to push her into this mess. I failed her in the worst possible way a father can fail his child, and I don't deserve to have her rescuing my sorry ass now."

Claire could feel herself being backed into a very dark corner. Her lizard brain had stopped whispering and was now jumping up and down, waving a red flag and shouting, *run*, run for our life.

Olivia took a couple of steps forward and stared into Claire's eyes. "Ms. Valentin, I know this isn't a perfect solution, but it's the only one that makes even the slightest bit of sense. I realize it's asking a lot, but I honestly don't see a way to resolve this situation without your help."

"All right...all right...how soon are they releasing him?"

"He has to be out of this room by 6pm today."

"They can't even give him until tomorrow morning?"

"According to the insurance protocols, without the surgery, he doesn't even warrant being in the room this long. The hospital administrators have actually been quite generous, especially considering..."

Claire rubbed her forehead. "Yeah, I get it. They're saints. And that gives me less than three hours to restructure my entire life."

"I have the utmost confidence that you'll get it all worked out," Olivia said brightly. Claire stifled the urge to strangle her. "And don't worry, you won't be completely on your own. I'll be coming out on a regular basis to conduct the mandated home visits."

"Fan-fucking-tastic," Claire said, half under her breath.

"Well, I'd better go check and make sure the nurse is working on those discharge papers. I'll be right back."

Claire rubbed her temples as Olivia hurried out the door.

"You sure you want to do this?" her father asked. Claire almost jumped out of her skin at the sound of his voice.

During the last few minutes, she had been so fixated on the problem of him, she had lost the sense that there was a human being behind all the drama and logistical bullshit.

"No Dad. To be honest, I'm not sure about any this. But it seems that neither one of us has a choice. You can't stay here, and I'll burn in Hippocratic Hell if I allow you go home by yourself. For right now, let's just worry about getting you back to your place. Tomorrow, we'll figure out what comes next."

Twenty minutes later, Olivia returned with a fistful of paperwork and a wheelchair. Ten minutes after that, they were rolling through the hospital lobby and out the front door.

Claire left Olivia to keep an eye on her father while she headed to the parking lot to retrieve the car. Her mind was on autopilot as she spotted the bright blue of her LeBaron in a far corner and steered toward it like a lighthouse beacon on a stormy night.

BRAAAWWWKKK! The sound of a horn and the squeal of locked up brakes blew through Claire's mental fog. She looked up in time to see a motorcyclist skimming by her, fighting to keep his bike from sliding out from underneath him. It took him a few seconds, but as Claire held her breath, he muscled the bike upright and rolled it to a safe stop against the curb.

"Sorry," she yelled.

The biker turned and flipped up the visor on his helmet. "Claire, are you okay?"

Shit, it was Joe Hottie, Male Nurse. And thanks to her wandering around with her head up her ass, she had almost caused him to dump his vintage red and black, leather-saddled Indian Chief.

"Zack! I'm so sorry!" she said, rushing toward him.

"It's okay, bike and biker are thankfully in one piece. Are you okay? You walked right out into the road without even looking. If I had been a semi truck, you'd be flatbread by now."

"It's been a helluva day. I was just getting the car to take Dad home, and I started thinking about everything I need to do..."

"Did you say you're taking your father home? You mean he's been discharged?"

"Yeah, I thought you knew. I assumed you were the nurse Olivia Hershel was working with to get the papers filled out."

"No, one of the other patients on the floor coded and I was hung up there until shift change. I'm surprised I didn't hear about it, though."

"I'm surprised there were no sounds of cheering or champagne bottles popping as we rolled down the hall."

"Hey, give us credit for having a little class...we wait until the former patient is legally off the property before the celebrating begins."

"Ah, so since he's still sitting on your front sidewalk, I'd better get my ass in gear so you can get to the party started."

Claire and Zack looked back toward the front doors where Olivia and Benjamin were staring and making hurry up motions.

"It's none of my business, Claire, and I know you're a professional, but are you going to be able to handle your father by yourself? Is the house at least set up for a wheelchair and everything that he's going to need?"

"No, it's not, but it will be. If the hospital had been able to keep him for even another day, I wouldn't be walking into traffic, but you gotta do what you gotta do. I'll do the best I can with him tonight, and then tomorrow I'll start hitting the phones again."

"Look, I don't have any plans for tonight. What if I escort you and your father home and at least help you get him settled in?" "Zack, that's incredibly generous of you, but I couldn't im-

pose..." "You're not imposing, I'm volunteering. In fact, I'm insisting.

Call it a professional concern for my patient's well being." "But you know what an asshole he can be. I can't promise he'll

be any better outside the hospital. In fact, if past experience is any indication, I can pretty much guarantee he'll be off the charts, pain in the ass-wise."

"That's okay. I'm not doing this for him. I'm doing it for my own piece of mind and as a courtesy, one caregiver to another."

"All right. Thank you."

"Let me park my bike, then I'll help you get him in the car. I'll follow you from there."

"Have you ever been out to The Fish Camp?"

"No, I'm not much of a sportsman. But from what I've heard, it's pretty close to paradise."

"Well, just be careful. The last time I was on the road to paradise, it was unpaved, rocky, and full of mud holes deep enough to suck your bike down whole."

CHAPTER THIRTEEN

Thanks to Zack, they got her father and his cumbersome full leg cast settled in the back seat of the LeBaron with a minimum of difficulty. Olivia was twitchy and seemed to be suffering from a gigantic bug up her backside, but Claire shrugged it off as the side effect of being forced to spend more than five minutes alone with her father.

"Do you remember where you're going, Claire?" her father called as they turned out of the hospital driveway and onto the main drag.

"Yep, we're good." Claire checked the rear view mirror and was pleased to see the red motorcycle right on their tail.

The most direct route to the Fish Camp took them through the downtown area and out to the northwest corner of town. She was surprised to see that-- other than an increase in cookie cutter McMansions and the corresponding decrease in wood and farmland-- not much had changed over the past two decades.

"I see you finally broke down and put up a sign for the place," Claire said as they slowed to turn at a rustic looking log sign with an arrow pointing toward the Camp.

"It's Tandy's idea. She calls it free advertising. I told her anything that cost me two grand doesn't fit my definition of free."

"Any chance she also talked you into getting the road fixed?"

"Nah, this keeps the yahoos from using it as a racetrack. And according to Tandy's website, it adds to the 'rural atmosphere'".

"Well, I hope your rural atmosphere doesn't rip out my shocks and undercarriage."

"Just go slow and swing over to the right when you stop in front of the gate. There's a nasty sinkhole left and center. Here, take the key."

Claire pulled the car over as instructed, wrestled the huge padlock open, and swung the gate far enough inward to allow the LeBaron to pass.

"Claire, don't worry about the gate, I'll close it behind us and catch up," Zack yelled over the rumble of his motor.

She raised her hand in thanks, slid back behind the wheel, and drove them onto Fish Camp property.

The sun wasn't down yet, but here, under the canopy of oak, pine and maple trees, it was already twilight. The narrow road between the gates and the lake wound, twisted and bounced through almost two miles of deep woods and marshland before opening up into the large gravel parking area in front of the Lodge. An even smaller dirt footpath continued on around the lake, but for anything with four wheels, the Lodge lot was the end of the line.

The Lodge was the Fish Camp's heart, a community center where her father held court, watched endless satellite sports, played host to his friends, and kept an eye and ear on everything that was going on in his fiefdom. From Memorial Day to Labor Day, it was also the check-in area for the summer cabin rentals: twelve small two room cottages, perched around the edges of the lake like pearls in a necklace. Fish Camp members and their families got first dibs, but there were always a fair number of out-of-towners and vaca- tioners among each season's weekly rental groups.

At this time of year, though, the Lodge's lot was deserted. Her father's house, her childhood home, was next door, to the left. There was a stone path that ran between the two buildings, but no easy way to maneuver the car close enough to her father's front door to make his transfer a painless one. Claire pulled the car in next to her father's rusted out K-5 Blazer and shut off the engine.

Claire stepped out of the car and surveyed the geography, trying to figure out how to best to get her father inside his own home. Besides the gravel walkway, there was also a set of steep, narrow and rail-less front stairs they would have to contend with.

"Problem?" asked Zack, walking up beside her.

"Not if we all sprout wings in the next five minutes." Claire trudged back to the car and stuck her head in the window. "Dad, just out of curiosity, how the hell did you plan on getting yourself into the house without help?"

"Didn't. Figured my best bet would be to give Mikey or whoever was driving the cab a few extra bucks, send them up to the Infirmary to grab a wheelchair and roll me into the Lodge for the time being. I've got all the comforts there-- kitchen, bar, recliner, big screen-- plus enough room to bumble around in. Not to mention that since the fucking zoning board made me build that fancy shitter for cripples, I might as well get my money's worth out of it."

"Good thinking, Dad. Should have come up with that one myself. Is the Infirmary locked?"

"Yep, like always. Here's the key to the Lodge. The Infirmary key is hanging with the rest of them on the wall in the office."

"Zack, if you'll stay and keep an eye on Dad, I'll go get the chair."

"No offense, Nursie, but I don't need a fucking babysitter, especially if all I'm doing is sitting here inside a goddamn car. I'd feel better if you went with Claire. It's been a long time since she's had to find her way around this place, and it's going to be dark soon."

"All right, Zack, let's go then. Wait, hold on a second." Claire popped the trunk and rooted around in it for a couple of seconds. "Here, take this," she said, handing her father a foot long black metal rod.

"What's this?"

"Telescoping walking stick. If you need us, slide it open and punch the horn. I left the key in the accessory position."

Claire and Zack trotted across the parking lot to the Lodge's large carved wooden doors. She hated to admit it, but she was glad her father had insisted that Zack go with her. She let them into the foyer and hit the bank of lights. If he had made any changes to the place, other than the mandated handicapped bathroom, she couldn't tell from here. It still looked like the ultimate fantasy man-cave that she remembered, complete with wood paneling, massive stone fireplace, exposed beams, oversized TV screens, a 20 foot pewter-topped mahogany bar, pool, poker, ping pong and chess tables, and tanned cow hide covering every surface meant to be used by the human buttocks.

Zack got lost in admiration about halfway across the room.

"Wow! This place is amazing. And I thought they were talking about the lake views when they called this place paradise."

Claire smiled, but it was automatic and forced. Outside, in the parking lot, even with her father in the back seat of her car, she could still tell herself that this was just a job, another call like the thousands of others she had been on, and keep her professional mask plastered in place.

From the minute she crossed the threshold into the building, though, she could feel the facade slipping. She was home. And home was where all the bad stuff happened.

She swallowed hard and felt her shirt collar tighten around her neck like it was choking her. She pulled it up and away, trying to loosen the constriction, but the feeling of pressure lingered.

She hurried around the bar and down the hall to the office. The wall with all the cabin keys on it was just inside the door, and the Infirmary key with the big red cross on it was hanging where it always was, on the lower right corner. *Unless he was using it*, her lizard brain whispered. *Unless he was in there with someone... or waiting there for her.*

She shook her head to clear it and tried to take a deep breath. "Everything okay back there, Claire?" Zack called. "Fine! Got it!" she said, forcing herself to grab the key and jam it into her pocket before bolting out the door.

CHAPTER FOURTEEN

"Okay, let's go," Claire said, slowing to an amble and trying to appear nonchalant and normal.

"Where's this Infirmary?" Zack asked.

"It's on the other side of the boathouse, the first cabin on this side of the lake."

Claire led Zack out the side door and up the path beside the dock. It was almost full dark, and they had to carefully pick their way up the loose stone path.

"You know, we used to have a camp back home in Norristown that was about this size. All I remember them having was an old First Aid kit with four band aids and a bottle of mercurochrome in it. A whole Infirmary seems..."

"A little over the top?"

"Well, yeah, maybe...unless it was like that camp up in Ashford that hosts sick kids. Kathy Anderson, one of the other RN's on the floor, volunteers up there for a week every summer."

"No, this has never been that kind of camp. Dad was a medic in Korea, and is obsessed about being prepared for the usual camper emergencies, like plague, volcanic eruption, nuclear winter. You know, the everyday stuff."

"Okay, well, there's a window into his personality that I'm not sure I needed to peek through."

"Welcome to my world. Here we are."

"Wow, that's a serious deadbolt."

"Can't be too careful. The woods are dripping with medical supply thieves." Claire fitted the key into the lock, hoping Zack didn't notice the way her hands were shaking.

"Well if this place is tricked out anything like the Lodge, I can't wait to see it."

Zack crowded behind her as she got the door open and slid

her hand along the wall, searching for the light panel. There was no way she was walking into that room in the dark. After fumbling for a few seconds, she found the switch, and the room's overhead fluorescents buzzed to life.

"Holy Hawkeye Pierce! This place is better outfitted than the first clinic I worked in."

"The wheelchair is probably still over there in the alcove with the backboards and water rescue stuff. We'd better grab it and get back to Dad. By now, he's probably wrestling a raccoon for the energy bars in the glove compartment."

"Hold on a sec, I have got to check this place out a little. Is that a Brewer exam table? Wow, it is. That's a nice piece of equipment. Cool, a Halogen light and a mobile magnifier! I guess splinters aren't a problem around here. And cabinet space...oh man, I'd give my left nut for this kind of storage space at the hospital."

"Yeah, it's great. Once we get back with the wheelchair, you guys can sit down over a cup of tea and debate stainless steel vs. plastic bedpans."

"Sorry. It's a vocational side effect, equipment envy. As a paramedic, I'd think you'd be familiar with the condition."

"Sure, yeah, equipment envy, all the time. Look, there's the damn chair. Let's just get out of here."

"Okay, okay. I'm right behind you."

* * * *

"What the hell happened to you two?" Valentin asked as they opened his door and got the chair positioned for the transfer. "I was beginning to think you were bear chow."

"No, Dad, no bears."

"Or that you stopped to tear off a piece, but since you were with Nursie there, eaten by wild animals seemed more likely."

"Dad!"

"Sorry, Mr. Valentin, it was my fault we took so long. I got caught up admiring your Infirmary. I was telling your daughter, you've got a better set-up than the clinic I worked at down in Philadelphia."

"Liked our little Infirmary did you?"

"Yes, sir. You've got an amazing combination of state-of-the-art and antique equipment in there."

"Yep, a little hobby of mine. Some of those pieces date back to the Civil War. I'm surprised that someone your age gives a shit about it, though. I'd pat you down to make sure you didn't 'borrow' anything, but I'm afraid you'd like it too much."

"Okay, Dad, enough. Let's get you inside."

With Zack's assistance, transferring her father from the car to his king-sized recliner inside the Lodge went fairly well. The old man grumped and complained, but no more so than anyone else with a freshly broken leg who was getting jostled around. He also seemed, temporarily at least, to lay off harassing Zack. He wasn't exactly polite, but he kept the "Nursie" crap to a minimum.

Once her father was ensconced, it took them another hour or so to rearrange the large room's floor plan to make sure he had all of life's necessities, like the perfect view of the big screen and a clear path to the bathroom. By 8pm, her father started complaining that he was hungry, so she checked the kitchen area and was pleasantly surprised to find that the handicapped bathroom wasn't the only upgrade he had made. She threw together three sandwiches, grabbed three glasses of ice tea, put them on a tray and headed back out to the main room.

As soon as she walked through the doorway, she could sense the tension, and one look at Zack's reddened face confirmed it. His jaw was clenched and his fingers were digging into the chair so deeply that his knuckles were white.

"What's going on in here?" she asked as she handed her father his plate and put the glass down on the table next to him.

"Nothing...just having a friendly little guy chat," her father said.

"Really?" Claire asked, setting the tray down on the table. She looked at Zack.

"Yep, just chatting," he said without looking at her. "You know Claire, it's getting pretty late. I have an early shift tomorrow, and I should probably get going so I can get some sleep."

"Okay...how about if I wrap your sandwich and you can take

it to go. It's the least I can do."

"Thanks, but I'm really not hungry. It would just be wasted on me."

"Are you sure?"

"Claire, if the man says he has to go, he has to go. Don't be clingy, girl. Men don't like that. Not even men like Nursie here. And don't forget, you'll have to follow him down to the gate to let him out. You've still got the key, right?"

"Yeah, Dad, it's right here," she said, patting her pocket.

"Great," Zack said, "Let's get going." Claire nodded, but Zack was already halfway across the room. By the time she got outside, he had jammed the helmet on his head and was revving his bike, discouraging all conversation.

He tore out of the parking lot and she followed, hoping for one last chance to talk at the gate, but when they reached it, their headlights revealed that it was already standing open, as if inviting him to please get the hell out. It was a message he obviously welcomed, blowing through it without even a flash of brake lights.

"What the fuck was that all about?" she asked out loud. Zack certainly wasn't the first person her father had driven away, but she couldn't imagine what kind of noxious horse shit he could have spewed in the few minutes she was in the kitchen that would have freaked him out that badly. He was a nurse, for God sakes.

It couldn't have been the homophobic crap. Her father had been slinging that garbage all day, and Zack had just let it roll off his back.

Her eyes focused on the metal barrier glittering in front of her. And what the hell was that gate doing open? Zack had stayed behind to close it after they had gone through, hadn't he? Maybe he'd had a premonition of the way the evening would go and left it open, just in case. Maybe he was the smart one. Maybe she should follow his example, hit the gas instead of the brakes, and not stop until she was back in Albany.

She gave it a full ten seconds of serious thought before slamming the stick in park and getting out to lock up for the night.

CHAPTER FIFTEEN

"What the hell did you say to Zack?" Claire yelled, storming back into the Lodge.

"Not a thing. Like I said, we were just chit-chatting."

"You said *something* to him, or he wouldn't have taken off like that."

"Face it, girl, you weren't his type. He probably just remembered that there was a hot cock waiting for him somewhere. You know how those boys are." He waved his hand like he was shooing a fly. "Just forget about the Fagola Angel of Mercy there. I'm sure he's already forgotten about you. On a much more important matter, I gotta take a wicked leak. How do we make that happen?"

Claire swallowed her anger and switched into automated care-taker mode. "It's up to you. Can you hold it long enough for me to get you to the bathroom or do you want the urinal?'

"I hate that damn piss jar, but I don't think I'll make it to the shitter in time."

"All right. I put it on the floor next to your chair. Let me get it for you."

Claire grabbed the plastic container, handed it to her father and turned away to give him some privacy.

"While you're doing that, I'll take the dishes back into the kitchen."

"Damn it. Claire, can you help me? My pants are caught on the top of the cast."

"Okay, hold on." She bent across him and reached down to where the cast was jammed up against his cut off pajama leg. As she fumbled with the fabric, he clamped his hand down over her arm with an iron grip.

"What the...?"

"Here's what you really want, girl," he said, dragging her hand to his crotch and rubbing it against his hard cock. She tried to pull away, but he squeezed her wrist until the carpel bones ground together.

"Let me go, you bastard."

"Not until we get a few things straightened out, and at least one thing softened up, if you catch my drift."

"Take your fucking hands off me, or I'll punch your lights out."

She had no sooner spit the words at him when a sharp blade bit into her neck and a female voice whispered in her ear. "I wouldn't recommend that."

"Claire, you remember Tandy O'Neil, your friend Olivia's sister? Tandy, I know you remember Claire."

"Damn straight I remember this bitch. She's the one that took off. Just up and left and broke her Daddy and Livvy's hearts. Didn't even say goodbye, fuck you or shit you later."

"Well Tandy, Claire is home now. And we'll just have to do everything in our power to make sure that she never leaves us again. Isn't that right?"

"Abso-fucking-lutely, Big Daddy."

"And I think she needs to start by showing her Daddy how sorry she is, and taking her medicine like when she used to be my good little patient."

"Do what your Daddy says, Sugar," Tandy said keeping the knife poised under her jaw with one hand and pushing Claire's head down into her father's lap with the other.

Thisisnthappening. Thisisnthappening. Thisisnthappening. Wake up. Wake up. You've had these dreams before. *Wake Up!*

Adrenalin surged through her body, but neither fight nor flight was a viable option. Her eyes spun in their sockets. Focus. Yes, find something to focus on...the pattern on her father's pajama bottoms were little fish, catfish she thought...yeah, definitely catfish, she could see the little whiskers. Catfish like the ones that live in the lake.

"Take your medicine! Take your medicine!" Tandy was chanting.

He forced himself into her mouth and Claire fought to keep her mind from slipping away. She had to think. She wasn't a helpless five year old girl any more. She gagged as he pushed deeper. The knife pressed harder against her skin and she could feel blood trickling down her neck and soaking into her collar.

Breathing through her nose, she struggled to keep from vomiting. His smell...sour and sharp like rotting cheese, and that hissing sound he always made...her eyes found the fish again and she began to drift. Her up and down motion made them swim, like they were in the lake, or down at the shore with the waves and the warm sun... little splashes of red, like wild roses dotting the shore line...

No. Claire snapped her mind back into the present. Splitting was not an option. Not here. Not now. She had to stay tethered to her body in order to save her own life. She was alone here with two psychos and no one was coming to her rescue.

Rescue. Training. She'd been a paramedic longer than she'd been his fucking victim. How would she act if this were a call? She'd been in some tight spots on the job before-domestics, shootings, first on the scene for a stabbing only to find out the perp was still in the house with the knife. She had survived, and she hadn't done it by allowing her mind to take a vacation to la-la land.

Focus, Claire. Appraise the situation. That was rule number one in EMS. She concentrated on ticking off her circumstances as they appeared at the moment:

Tandy would kill her and not think twice about it, but her father was running the show, at least for the moment.

If he had wanted her dead, they wouldn't have gone to all this trouble to accomplish it. Therefore...

He had something else in mind; and if past experience was any indicator, it probably had to do with keeping her alive and useable for as long as possible.

What it basically came down to was that while it sucked to be her, the good news was that they probably weren't going to kill her right away...of course that was also the bad news.

Her jaws ached as he increased his tempo. His fingers felt like they were drilling through the back of her skull as he crushed her face into his groin. She couldn't breathe. Panic set her nerves on fire and she squirmed and bucked, not caring about the knife, or the blood, or that her struggling was only intensifying his pleasure. With a final thrust he exploded down her throat and collapsed back in his chair, her head still locked in his steel grip.

"Good girl," he panted. He dropped his hands as his shrunken cock slithered out her mouth. "That was real nice. You always had a special talent for taking your oral injections."

"My turn! My turn!" Tandy shouted.

CHAPTER SIXTEEN

Tandy grabbed Claire by the arm and pulled her to a standing position. She kept the knife in her right hand and used her left to paw at Claire's breasts.

"Don't worry, Tandy honey, you'll get your chance...you'll get plenty of chances. Now that Claire is back for good, we'll have all the time in the world to play, won't we, girl?"

"My job...they know where I am. They'll send the police if I'm not there for my shift tomorrow."

"Liar, liar, now I get to set your ass on fire!" Tandy squealed in a childish sing-song. "Isn't that the rule, Big Daddy?"

"Yes, it is, baby girl. I guess Claire's forgotten what the punishment for telling fibs is around here. But that's okay. We'll refresh her memory."

"I...I'm not lying..."

"And lying about lying is another twenty strokes! Keep going, bitch, and Big Daddy's going to let me beat your ass clean off."

"That's right, Tandy, but first things first, remember?"

"Yes, sir."

"So what the fuck are you waiting for? Show me." Tandy grinned, turned to Claire and bellowed in her face. *"Strip, Bitch!"*

Claire stood swaying on her feet like a punch-drunk boxer. She tried to raise her hands to undo the buttons on her shirt, but it was as if she was wearing large, weighted oven mitts. After a few fumbling attempts, Tandy lost patience and ripped the front of her shirt open, pulled it off her arms and threw it on the floor.

"Stand still or I'll slice your tits off. You want something done right...," she grumbled. Using the knife, Tandy cut the rest of the clothes off her body until Claire was naked, except for her socks and sneakers. Retrieving her underwear from the floor, Tandy used her panties to tie her hands together behind her back and then used her bra to secure her ankles. When she was completely immobilized, Tandy pushed her backwards into one of the leather recliners. She then went through Claire's clothes, pulling out her phone, car keys, Infirmary and gate keys and transferring them to her own pockets.

"Don't worry about getting comfortable. You won't be there long. I'll be right back." Tandy walked over, planted a kiss on the top of her father's head and headed out of the room. "Don't talk about me too much."

"Isn't she unbelievable?" he asked after watching Tandy sashay out the door. "She was always my favorite of the camp kids, but who knew she'd be so much fun as a grown up? She called me after she moved back here to talk about doing some P.R. for the Camp. I wasn't too hot on the idea, but she talked me into meeting with her and boom, it was like lighting up an old grill with gasoline.

"And she's so fucking creative...not to mention the best age-appropriate piece of ass I've ever had." He was gushing like a teen-ager rhapsodizing over his first crush. "The things that girl comes up with are just balls to the wall amazing. Like figuring out how to use my little slip and fall to get you back here. I swear that girl's an evil genius. I think I'm in love.

"Of course it helped that you're such a gullible little sap. I can't believe you actually bought the whole Meth-Monster-mea-culpa- courage-to-heal bullshit that I laid on you. I bet you even believed I really used to cook up batches of tweek in that old stor-age shed.

"One thing you were right about, though. Those body parts in the swamp definitely weren't your Momma's Halloween deco-rations. Come to think of it though, they might have actually *been* your Momma." This struck him as especially funny, and he laughed until tears ran down his face and he had difficulty catch-ing his breath.

Claire knew he wanted her to respond, but she wasn't about to give him the satisfaction. Instead, she concentrated on trying to reposition herself in the chair. But between her restraints and the leather sticking to her naked skin, she was like a butterfly pinned to a mounting board.

And now that he had regained his composure, he was obviously enjoying the display. Even in the low light, she could see his eyes glowing as they roamed over her body. "Not bad for...what are you now, almost 40, right?" Claire didn't bother to tell him she would be 38 next month and he didn't wait for her answer.

"I see you lost that little bit of chub you had just after your titties came in, but hey. If Tandy prunes your puss patch, maybe puts your hair up in pigtails, and I squint just right, you might be worth doing."

Claire shuddered involuntarily. Words. They're just words, she told herself. *No, they're promises*, the lizard whispered. *And if you don't make a stand soon, you'll never leave this place.*

Breathe. Concentrate. There has to be a way out. He's got a broken leg, for God's sake. And the only weapon Tandy has shown so far is the knife. Dangerous as hell close in, but if she could get some distance on them, she might at least have a chance.

CHAPTER SEVENTEEN

"Doctor, Doctor, I'm in the mood...to be lewd, rude, and wildly screwed!" Tandy sang out as she banged back in through the Lodge doors, carrying two large duffel bags.

"Jay-zus, girl, it looks like you cleaned the whole Infirmary out."

"Well, you said to bring down anything I thought we could have fun with...and there were just so many goodies to choose from, I couldn't help myself."

"You've always been a little toy piggy, haven't you?"

Tandy dropped the bags next to Valentin's recliner and began snorting and waggling her ass. Claire's stomach flipped as she watched the twisted display of familiarity and affection.

"What did piggy bring me? Show Big Daddy what his good little piggy brought him."

Tandy zipped open the bags and gently placed them in Valentin's lap for his perusal. He and Tandy put their heads together as they sorted through the contents, laughing softly together and glancing over at their victim. Claire caught flashes of gynecological instruments, rubber tubing, sex toys, latex gloves, bondage gear and an black case she knew held a set of surgeon's tools liberated from the Auschwitz concentration camp.

Claire closed her eyes and tried to concentrate on breathing deeply and keeping herself present. She hadn't seen some of those items since she was a child, since her father used to make her take a growth check every Monday evening. Year round, Mondays were the quietest days at the Camp; the few members that were around were usually too busy working off their weekend hangovers to care what old Val was doing locked in the Infirmary with his daughter.

He would make her take off all her clothes and put on one of those hospital johnnies that opened up in the back. She used to close her eyes back then, too, but like now, it only shut out the visual images, it didn't keep out the clank of the instruments hitting the metal tray or the smell of the peppermint castile soap and rubber tubing or the shock of the cold lubricating jelly. And even screwing her eyes shut as tight as possible didn't keep the light from the flashbulbs out. At least when he got the camera out, she knew it was almost over, for this week anyway. Pose this way, put your hands there, show me this, and then finally, be a good little patient and take your medicine...and then she could get dressed, go home and have something to eat.

That was her schedule every Monday, from her earliest memory to the day she got her first period. When she was in Kindergarten and her mother had still been around, she had asked her why Daddy did that to her every week. She told her she had asked her friend Lilly if her Daddy checked her like that, and Lilly told her no, no one was allowed to touch her pee-pee except her Mommy and Doctor Scott.

Her mother had slapped her hard across the face and told her to never, ever, ever tell anyone what went on in the family. She said it was nobody's business but our own, and if Daddy ever found out Claire told someone, he'd give her a lot more than a check up... and that she'd get in big trouble, too.

Her mother had sent her to bed that night without her supper. And when she woke up in the morning, her mother was gone. She searched the house and then the whole Camp, but she couldn't find her.

Hours later, and hoarse from calling for her Mommy, she found her father in the Lodge and begged him to tell her where her mother was. He squatted down, looked her in the eye, and told her that her mother had gone away and it was all Claire's fault. She couldn't stand having such a bad girl for a daughter, so she took off and was never coming back.

Then he stood up and strode out of the building leaving her five-year-old self, broken and sobbing, standing in almost exactly the same spot where she lay now.

A shifting of light on the other side of her closed lids brought Claire's attention back to the present. She opened her eyes and saw a huge meat hook was now dangling about six feet in front of her. A rope had been slung over one of the ceiling's exposed beams and tied off to the bar.

The motion of the hook was hypnotic as it swung gently back and forth. Claire didn't take her eyes off of it until Tandy grabbed her by her breasts and dragged her to her feet.

"If it were up to me, I'd make you ride this bad boy until it split you open twat to tongue, but Big Daddy has something else in mind." Tandy moved behind her, and she could feel the knife cutting through the cloth around her wrists.

"Put your hands in front of you." Tandy took a roll of duct tape out of the pile of toys and wrapped it around Claire's wrists a dozen times before tearing it off. She then took the hook, pulled it between Claire's bound hands and jerked it upwards to seat it.

"Now don't you move...we're going to find out if you can fly."

The rope had been looped around the rail on the bar. Tandy walked to the bar, untied the rope and gave it a pull that yanked Claire's arms up above her head. Tandy's second, stronger pull moved Claire's body up so that her toes barely touched the floor as they scrambled for purchase.

"That's high enough for now, Tandy," Valentin called. "Tie her off and get that spreader locked between her feet. And don't forget to put the tarp down, I just had the floors refinished, and I don't want any body fluids fucking them up. "

"Yes, sir."

It only took Tandy a few minutes to swap out the ankle bindings for the cuffs and bar. Claire tried to extend her toes, catch hold of a little piece of floor in order to keep the pressure off her wrists and shoulders for as long as possible. But every time she found an almost comfortable balance point, Tandy would knock her off and set her swinging.

"Now, isn't that a pretty presentation, Tandy? She's completely immobilized, but we don't have to give up full body access. This is what I mean about thinking things through."

"You're right, Big Daddy, I never should have doubted you. Do you want to punish me?"

"Yes and your punishment will be that you'll have to wait and go second. We'll do what I want to do to her first."

"Okay, where do you want me to start?"

"Shave her. Once you get rid of her snatch thatch, we can see how much my favorite patient has grown in the past 20 years."

"I thought I was your favorite, Big Daddy," Tandy pouted as she pulled a straight razor from one of the bags.

"You always be my favorite camp kid, Tandy, but remember Claire is my daughter. She's got my blood, and that means that she's more like me than any other person on this planet. Not to mention all the time we had to play together after I got rid of that stupid cunt that shat her out."

Claire felt the cold metal scraping against her vulva and the rough fingers poking and pulling at her labia, but it was her father's words ringing in her head that turned her blood to ice. He had got- ten rid of her mother. He had made her mother disappear and no one had ever cared.

She struggled to remember what her mother had even looked like. She had been five...that had been almost 33 years ago. She remembered the slap, and she remembered her mother's rough, red hands, bony and strong.

But what about her face? Were her mother's eyes hazel like hers? Was her hair straight or curly? Had Claire ever seen her smile? She couldn't remember. Her father was so much larger than life. He took up so much space inside her head there wasn't room for anyone or anything else. Her memory was like a photograph with her father, in painfully sharp focus, filling up the foreground.

And then there was her mother, the ghostly, blurred figure in the background.

CHAPTER EIGHTEEN

Claire stopped feeling her arms not long after the big grand-father clock in the foyer chimed 4am. By that time, she had lost count of the number of times she had been invaded, skewered, poked, distended, fucked, injected, lashed and displayed. After Tandy shaved her, she followed her father's directions and subject-ed her to a kinkster style Ob/Gyn exam complete with speculums, dilators, retractors, clamps and all the other medical tools he loved to play with. He had enjoyed himself immensely, finally calling Tandy away from Claire to assist him through to his happy ending.

And then it was Tandy's turn. While Claire's father's was still working off the same Dr. Mengele playbook he had always used, Tandy's predilections were less easy to pigeonhole. The common denominator was the obvious wettie she got from the infliction of pain, but there was so much more to it than that. She was fascinated by Claire's skin and fixated on finding innovative ways to breach it.

Once Valentin gave Tandy the okay, the first thing she did was relocate the big mirror from above the hearth over next to Claire so she wouldn't miss a moment of the action. Then she moved on to the main event and pulled out a box of hypodermic needles sans syringes. One at a time, she inserted them into the meat of Claire's buttocks until, like a child's light box toy, the multicolored plastic end caps formed a colorful design. It took Tandy over an hour to place all the needles just so and then photograph her mas-terpiece, but that wasn't the end of it. After the final needle was seated, Tandy took one of the ping-pong paddles from the nearby table and proceeded to beat the needles flush into her skin.

The pain was more vicious than anything that Claire had ever experienced. It was like being attacked by a swarm of wasps that were stinging her from inside out. This was the "setting her ass on fire" punishment Tandy had promised her earlier for lying. And after Tandy had delivered the ten preliminary and twenty extra strokes, she finished up the session by laboriously pulling out each of the needles using a viciously fanged office staple remover.

By the time she was done, blood was seeping from all of Claire's wounds, dribbling down her legs and pooling on the floor underneath her. The gore seemed to only add to Tandy's enjoyment of the scene, though, as she and Valentin engaged in a frenzied, animalistic 69 session that left them temporarily satiated and Claire hanging in state of twilight consciousness.

The person-- the essence of who Claire believed she really was-- floated inside her skull as if it were a sensory depravation chamber. It was an old survival trick. When the pain in her body became unbearable, she unlatched the secret trap door in the roof of her mouth, climbed up inside her head and slammed it shut behind her. Her spirit stayed there, locked away and completely divorced from her body, until it was safe to go back.

This time, though, she couldn't imagine it ever being safe again.

She raised her eyelids slightly and peeked out from under her eyelashes. Her head was hanging down and the only thing in her vision field was the blue tarp covered in congealing splotches of body fluids. Her ears picked up movement and soft voices behind her, but she didn't dare give them any sign that she was alive, let alone conscious.

"Is she still breathing?" Claire heard her father ask.

"Can't tell from this angle, but there's one way to find out. Are you done draining the dragon?"

"Yeah, here."

Claire held her breath and tried to look as unresponsive as possible. The sound of Tandy's bare feet slapping against the hardwood floor changed to a wicking sound as she crossed over onto the tarp and stepped up behind her.

"Wakey-wakey piss and bakey!" Tandy yelled. Claire felt the warm fluid land on her back and turn into hot acid as it seeped into the open wounds on her backside. She tried to control herself but the pain was too much and she screamed like a rabbit caught in a wood chipper.

"She's alive," Tandy said, grabbing a fistful of Claire's hair and jerking her head back. "And it looks like she was trying to play possum on us, too."

"Tsk. Tsk. Tsk. Not the best way to start a bright new day, daughter dear."

"Can I punish her again, Big Daddy, can I please?" Tandy asked.

"Yes, but not until after you rustle us up some breakfast. I'm starving and we'll need to keep up our strength if we're going to have a repeat of yesterday's festivities."

"And while you're at it, do you think I could get a cup of coffee?" a female voice called from the back doorway.

Claire, her father and Tandy's heads all whipped around in unison

"Olivia, oh thank God...!" Claire said.

CHAPTER NINETEEN

"Big Sis, it's about time you showed up," Tandy called out.

"Olivia, Jay-zus, don't startle an old man like that." Valentin said, lowering the semi-auto pistol that had materialized in his hand. "You almost met Mr. TT-33 up close and personal."

"Olivia?" Claire choked out.

"Oh look, Sis, the bitch is confused," Tandy said.

Olivia crossed the room and pushed her face into Claire's until their noses were less than an inch apart and she was staring deeply into Claire's eyes. "See, I told you, Tandy. She never was very bright."

"Olivia, you...you're...you knew?"

"Y-Y-Y-Yessssss I knew," she said, spraying spittle all over Claire's face. "I helped plan the whole operation, you stupid cunt. Whew!" Olivia stepped back a few paces and fanned her nose. "You are one disgusting pile of dog shit. I don't know how anyone can stand to be in the same room with you."

"Don't worry, it's temporary," Tandy said. "I was planning on throwing her into the lake after breakfast for a rinse off. Or maybe, if she continues to be such a lying pain-in-the-ass sack of shit, we'll just cut our losses and toss her directly into the swamp with the rest of the carcasses."

"With or without the cuffs on?"

"Depends how nice she is to Big Daddy and me in the meantime."

"Well, it sounds like you've got a full day of fun planned."

"Can you stay and play for awhile?"

"Sure, I've got some time. If it's okay with Big Daddy, of course."

"The more the merrier," Valentin said, giving himself a big

stroke and smiling broadly.

"Sounds like a plan then. How about if you and I get some coffee going, and we'll see what we can whip up in that nice new kitchen of yours for breakfast."

"Great, and that'll give me a chance to give you a tour of the renovations. Did I tell you we're going to be catering parties now? Wait until you see the new stove. Everything is restaurant quality. We even upgraded to a walk in freezer and cooler. We'll make a mint this summer on graduation parties and weddings alone."

The two sisters walked back toward the kitchen, chatting and laughing like Olivia had popped by to borrow a cup of sugar. Minutes later, the smell of freshly brewing coffee wafted in, accompanied by the clinking and banging sounds of a meal being prepared.

Claire tried to wrap her mind around Olivia's presence, her lies and machinations and her obvious rage. But no matter how hard she tried, she couldn't make any sense out of it. Meanwhile, the Cleaver Family Reunion continued to play itself out in front of her while her naked, bloody body swung gently in the morning breeze.

"Frozen waffles or pancake mix, Big Daddy?" Tandy asked, poking her head into the room.

"Is it the dry mix or that batter in a jug stuff?"

"Jug."

"Definitely waffles then. And how about trotting some of that coffee out here instead of just cock-teasing me with the smell?"

"Coming right up!" Tandy said, disappearing back into the kitchen.

More banging around, and Olivia hurried out carrying a big, steaming mug. "I've got it, Tandy," she yelled back over her shoulder. "You just make sure those waffles don't burn. Here you go, Big Daddy, cream, two sugars, right?" she asked, standing over him.

He smiled and nodded, and as he reached out for the cup, Olivia dumped the steaming liquid dead center on his crotch. Valentin bellowed in pain, grabbed his poached testicles and wrenched his body back and forth, trying in vain to escape the burning beverage.

Olivia lunged forward and jammed her right hand into his chest. There was a loud *zzzittt* sound, an electrical flash, and he collapsed back in his chair, his head lolling off to the side.

"The gun, Olivia! Get his gun!" Claire yelled.

"On it!" Olivia said, stuck her hand underneath Valentin's limp body and rooted around until she located the firearm and pulled it out. She checked the safety and the clip and slid it into the waist- band of her pants.

"Where's Tandy?" Claire asked

"Safely locked up in the pantry. I zapped her when she went in to get the sugar for his coffee."

"Brilliant. I knew it didn't make any sense that you were involved in all of this. Now, please get me down from here. And tell the cops to bring an ambulance with them. I don't think I'll be able to walk out of here on my own."

Olivia hurried over to the bar, loosened the rope and as carefully as she could, lowered Claire to the ground. As her feet came in full contact with the floor, Claire tried to hold her weight up, but her legs folded underneath her and she ended up flat on her back, her legs and arms not responding to the frantic messages from her brain.

"Here, let me help you sit up," Olivia said, kneeling down next to her.

"No, let me just lie here for a few minutes until the circulation comes back. I would appreciate you getting me out of this duct tape and bondage gear though."

Olivia unbuckled the ankle cuffs and pulled the spreader bar out from between Claire's legs. "I don't have scissors for the tape, but there must be some in the kitchen. Hold tight, I'll go get them."

"Hurry up, we don't know how long it'll be before he starts coming around."

"Oh, don't worry about that," Olivia said, veering off her path to stop by and hit Valentin with another long zap of from her stun gun. "He won't be going anywhere for a while."

Olivia retrieved the scissors and spent the next few minutes cutting Claire out of her restraints, wrapping her in blankets and muscling her dead weight up into the wheelchair that she had rolled over.

"There. Now you're almost presentable. "

"Yeah, I'm sure Paxton's finest will think I'm adorable. And speaking of the devils, we'd better make that 911 call. It's going to be tough enough to get the cops to believe what happened here without making them wonder why we didn't call for help the minute we got the chance."

"Face it, Claire. The cops are never going to believe all of this. They're never going to believe us over their best buddy here," Olivia said walking back over to Valentin.

"You don't know that for sure."

"Claire, I was born here. I've lived here all my life. I know how this town works, and so do you, if you'll get your head out of your goody-goody Girl Scout ass and admit it. The cops are never going to believe that their good friend Benjamin Valentin was responsible for any of this. Hand him over to them and he'll talk and spin and twist it around and end up blaming Tandy for everything. By the time he gets done, he'll have them convinced that he's the victim here. Shit, he'll probably find a way to make us out to be accomplices or something."

"Olivia, I know you're worried about Tandy, but we have to call the cops. Look, it's obvious she's sick. If they arrest her, they'll make her see a doctor, and maybe she'll finally be able to get the help she needs."

"*No.* The only help that Tandy needs is to get away from *this.* Zap. *Asshole.* Zap. *Right.* Zap. *Here.*"

"Olivia! Stop! You're going to kill him!"

"You're absolutely right. Killing him now would be much to good for him. Much too easy. That's why we are *not* going to call the cops. Instead, you and I are going to spend a little time getting up close and personal with our favorite pervert here. We're going to have a little fun with him. And finally, we're going to make him disappear."

"Olivia, come on. You know I can't do that. You know *you* can't do that. Let's just call the cops and let them deal with him. Tandy will be okay. I'll even testify that she wasn't the one responsible, it was all him."

"Well, you're right about the responsibility part...it was all him. And because it was all him, there's no way in hell I'm going to let him talk his way out of it or have his cop buddies or a bunch of lawyers, cover this up or get him off the hook, like they always do. *This* time he's going to pay, and you and Tandy and I are the ones he owes."

"Olivia, I can't be part of this. Look, I understand how you feel. But if you do this, you'll be no better than he is."

"Yeah, that's always the party line isn't it? Bastards like him get to do whatever they want, to whoever they want, but when it's time for his victims to get their justice, they hand you a pile of that self-righteous lowering-yourself-to-his-level bullshit instead."

"If you kill him, you'll be just as responsible..."

"He's the only one here who's responsible for this situation. He *created* this situation, and he's also responsible for creating whatever monsters we've become because of it."

"I'm no monster, Olivia."

"Yeah, you are. You just refuse to admit it. It scares the shit out of you that it's there, right under your perfectly crafted surface. You've spent the last twenty years running away and hiding from it, but the truth is, the one thing you're the most afraid of has been right there inside of you the whole time, hasn't it?"

"You need help, Olivia. Let me help you."

"No, let me help *you*." Olivia grabbed the handles on the back of the wheelchair, spun her around and pushed her to her father's recliner. "I think it's time we threw your inner monster a little coming-out party...and we're going to kick it off by letting you give your father a little more electro-shock therapy."

"No, Olivia. I won't do it, and there's nothing and no one on this earth that can make me," Claire said, squirming around and trying to lift herself out of the chair.

"Sit down," Olivia ordered, clamping a hand on her shoulder. "No one, huh?" Olivia pulled a photograph out of her pocket and shoved it in front of Claire's face. "How about her?"

It took Claire a second to realize what she was looking at. When she did, she tried to turn away, but Olivia wouldn't let her. "Remember her? *Look* at her. Look at you."

CHAPTER TWENTY

Olivia was right. The little girl in the picture was her, at age five or six. The picture had been taken from above. It was crisp and clear and she could see every detail. The tears streaming down her face. The terror in her eyes. The way her mouth stretched out of shape as she struggled to swallow her father's cock.

Olivia grabbed her hand, pressed the palm-sized stun gun into it, and pushed it into her father's groin.

"Hit the button, Claire. Give him a good long blast. Think of all the times he did that to you. You were a little girl, and he called it taking your medicine, but he was fucking a sweet, precious, five- year-old girl's face. Your face, Claire. Do it, Claire, do it!"

Claire's hand trembled and tears rolled down her cheeks, but she shook her head. "I can't."

Olivia reached back into her pocket, took out a stack of photographs and let them flutter down into Claire's lap. "You weren't the only one. We weren't the only *ones*. I found the pictures... hundreds, maybe thousands of them. There were a dozen shelves hidden behind a false wall in his basement. The photos were stored in albums, but there were also shelves of videos, audiotapes, CD's, DVD's, you name it, along with two high end lap tops tricked out with all sorts of multi-media editing and production software.

"When I checked the computers out, I found out he had digitized his whole collection and was posting and selling them on the Internet. He's got a sophisticated portal website, and it looks like he's been running it for years. His fellow perverts sign up and, for a monthly membership fee, they can download whatever or whoever floats their boats.

"I got into the site and I saw his inventory. Images of you and me and Tandy and too many others to even recognize...and every month, he adds new sets of snapshots."

Claire's eyes widened and rolled upward as her finger found the slide button and slammed it forward. Her father's body jumped against her hand and she could smell the piss and shit leaking out of him.

"Again. Hit him again."

"It might be too much for him, Olivia."

"Do you think that thought ever crossed *his* mind when we were the ones being tortured?"

No, it didn't, not once, the lizard whispered. Photographs. Taking her medicine. Monday nights in the Infirmary. Internet child porn site. The Swamp. Getting rid of the stupid cunt that shat her out. Claire felt as if a confetti cannon stuffed with images of abuse had exploded inside of her skull.

She punched the button forward again, and in that moment, heard herself utter an almost inhuman scream, a deep guttural keening of rage and pain and grief as she watched him jiggle and seize.

"Now that's what I'm talking about," Olivia said.

Amazingly, the bastard was still alive. Claire could see the involuntary contractions of his hands as his body struggled to absorb this last round of shocks.

"Felt good, didn't it?" Olivia asked.

All Claire could manage was a nod, but inside, what she was experiencing was more astonishing than the most intense orgasm she had ever had. Every nerve ending in her body hummed and sparked. Her mental fog lifted, and it was as though she was seeing the world for the first time. It was fucking amazing.

In one moment, every thought and emotion she had kept locked down all these years had broken free and swept her away like a paper boat in a tidal wave. The lizard wanted more. *She* wanted more. She wanted to tear him apart with her teeth, tongue fuck his brain and douche with his blood. She wanted to cut a hole in his chest and set his heart on fire while it was still beating. And his cock… she would spend a week slicing it into millimeter thick strands and then make him floss with it.

Olivia watched as her newly tapped emotions blazed across Claire's face and lit up her eyes. She smiled and whispered, "Wel- come to the world, Monster Queen."

"More." Claire choked out. "I want to hurt him more. I want him to suffer. I want him to beg me to kill him."

"Good. And now that we're on the same page, we can get on with it."

"How?"

"First, let's get him out of that chair. He needs to know what it feels like to hang out with us for awhile, don't you think?"

"Abso-fucking-lutely."

"Have you recovered enough to help me do little furniture rearranging?"

"I don't know, let's see." Claire kicked up the foot rests on the wheelchair and slowly pushed herself to a standing position. The photographs tumbled out of her lap and scattered around her like fall leaves. She had a moment where she felt faint and unbalanced, but snapped back on purpose when she caught a movement out of the corner of her eye and realized her supposedly-unconscious father's right hand was worming its way down into the side of his chair.

"Looking for this, asshole?" Olivia called out, holding the weapon up where he could see it.

"Just scratching an itch on my poor broken leg," he answered with a smarmy smile.

"Funny you should mention your leg. Claire and I were just discussing that we think it's time you had a little physical therapy. We're going to get you up and moving around. After all, you don't want that leg to go bad on you."

"Here's the only one leg I want either of you bitches anywhere near," he answered, grabbing himself and wincing.

"Forgot that Olivia boiled your balls there, *Dad*?"

"Shit, that was a sprinkling of holy water compared to what's coming down the road at you two."

"Yep, definitely time for a little PT. Here, Claire. Take Tandy's work shirt to put on for now, and we'll get your father packaged up and ready to move. I'll be in charge of patient cooperation," she said stepping closer and leveling the pistol at his head.

Claire carefully slipped into the long-sleeved, long-tailed flannel, picked the duct tape up off the coffee table and proceeded to wrap her father's wrists the same way that Tandy has bound hers.

When they were sure he was properly restrained, Olivia holstered the gun, repositioned the hook and rope over the beam above them, and Claire secured her father to it.

Olivia yanked down on the rope and, as her father rose into the air, Claire shoved the chair out of the way, then helped Olivia tie the rope off to the leg of the pool table.

"Perfect," Olivia said as she inspected Valentin's dangling body. "Except for one thing. I think we need to see a little more skin, don't you, Claire?"

"Way ahead of you," Claire said, snapping the scissor blades open and shut as she walked around him. It occurred to her that the last time she had been this close to him, he had been 58 years old. To her teenaged self, he had been a concrete block of a man- all hard, flat, angular planes and surfaces, from the top of his military brush cut to the razor crease in his work pants.

She scrutinized him up and down, but she had to admit that the intervening years hadn't affected him much. His jug ears might be slightly larger, and he might have acquired a hint of a potbelly. But all in all, with the exception of the bulky cast and the catfish pajamas, he still looked like he could crush coal into diamonds with his bare hands.

"Shut up and do whatever you're gonna do. You think I'm weak like you? You think I'm going to cry and beg and plead like all of you do? Boo hoo you hurt my little poopie hole. Boo hoo, I don't wanna take my medicine, it tastes yucky. Wah Wah Wah. Fuck you both. Fuck you all. You don't know what pain is, but I'm sure as shit gonna educate you bitches soon enough."

"Thanks for the offer, Dad, but I've already got a master's degree from that particular school... and now I think it's time I returned the favor."

Claire punched the scissors through the fabric of his T-shirt and proceeded to cut through his clothing and, in some particularly sensitive spots, a layer or two of his skin as well. By the time she had stripped him completely, angry red tracks studded with droplets of blood crisscrossed his body like strings of Mardi Gras beads. Even the massive American eagle that stretched across his chest wept dark tears. "That all you twats got?" her father asked.

"Oh, give it a fucking rest," Olivia answered, slapping a strip of duct tape across his mouth before giving him a spin and a push, briefly turning him into the world's ugliest whirly-gig. "I'm bored with your bullshit already."

CHAPTER TWENTY-ONE

"Oh...looky what we've got over here," Claire said, spotting the two duffel bags Tandy had brought down from the Infirmary. "There must be a few toys left in there that they didn't get around to using on me. Let's see if we can find something nice and ironic."

"Hold on a sec. I've got a better idea." Olivia said. "Those toys were his idea, right?"

"Yeah, he sent Tandy up to the Infirmary with a list. Ah...I see where you're going. This play doctor shit is HIS idea of a good time."

"Exactly. I think it's time he got a taste of life on the other side of equation."

"Damn straight."

"After all, we all have our little kinks and preferences and... interests, don't we? Take me, for example. When I about five years old, this asshole who ran a summer camp got me alone, sat me down and told me that there was this awful, terrible medical thing wrong with me. He said I had broken my pussy by playing with it too much. He told me that if my parents or anyone else found out about it, they'd kick us out of Camp and send me away to a special hospital for really bad little girls. When I started to cry, he said he could fix me, but I had to do everything he told me to and never, ever tell anyone about it.

"I was so scared and embarrassed, I did whatever he said. I hated all the pictures and the examinations and having to take medicine all the time. It got so bad, I'd start throwing up a month before school ended, just from worrying about what he was going to do to me this year.

"The *only* thing that made me feel better, and made me forget him and his touchy, peeky, feely bullshit for even a little while, was fire. I would steal those little wooden matches from the tin on the mantle, sneak into the bathroom, take off all of my clothes and hold the lit match against my skin.

"The pain used to take my breath away. It hurt like hell, but it was a good hurt. It was a relief, like I was burning away all the dirty, filthy badness that was inside of me. And as long as I could concentrate on the pain, I didn't have to think about him.

"And then, one year I went back to Camp and he left me alone. He just wasn't interested in me any more. But I never stopped being interested in fire. Even all these years later, it still calms me down and makes me feel clean and good...and I think it's only fair that I share that special feeling with him, especially since he's responsible for this little passion of mine in the first place."

Claire reached out and patted Olivia's arm. "Sounds more than fair to me. Do you want me to find you some wooden matches or...?"

"No, I saw something even more interesting in the kitchen when Tandy and I were farting around with breakfast. They have one of those culinary blowtorches like the chefs use to make *crème brulee*."

"Sweet. I say go for it."

The women took off for the kitchen. And as they passed her father, Claire could swear she saw the tiniest spark of fear in his eyes.

"Oh, yeah. This will do nicely," Olivia said, digging her new toy out of one the island drawers. "It's a beauty, too. Brand new, full of butane, and ready to caramelize. You know, I heard that some of these mini-torches are good for something like 70 hours, and burn as hot as 2500 degrees Fahrenheit."

"Wow, considering two seconds in 150 degree water will give you a third degree burn... just out of professional curiosity alone, I can't wait to see what happens to skin at that temperature."

"I'd say we have an obligation to the furtherance of medical knowledge to check it out, then."

Claire and Olivia were giggling like schoolgirls by the time they got back to where their captive was hanging.

"Oh Dad...remember all those toys of yours you were so

gen erous in sharing with us? Well, Olivia found one she wants to share with you."

Olivia held up the eight inch silver and black torch in front of him and tapped the red ignition button until a triangular blue flame blossomed at the end of the shiny metal nozzle.

Valentin's eyes shifted between the women and the torch. For the first time, that haughty look of superiority was gone, and beads of sweat were popping up along his hairline. Olivia noticed it, too, and smiled.

"So Claire. In your professional opinion, what would happen to say, a human penis, if it were to come in contact with a 2500 degree blowtorch flame?"

"Well, I'd have to double check with medical control, but I believe the technical term for that situation would be a fucking weenie roast."

"And how long do you think it would it take to get said weenie fired up to roasting temperature?"

"I've never treated a blowtorch injury myself, but I would take an educated guess that even a micro-second's worth of contact would melt straight through all the dermal layers, probably leaving a blackened, gaping hole that would most likely become infected and eventually require amputation."

"What if the burn were more extensive?"

"Oh, I'd say death would be inevitable...and it would be a really nasty one, too."

"Well, let's keep that as an option. But what if I wanted to start with something a little less radical. Like, say I use said blowtorch to burn off some of this repulsive pelt he's sporting here?"

"It'd probably take a little trial and error to get the distance right. But I bet you could get pretty good at singeing his hair off without doing more than a first-degree burn's worth of damage to the skin underneath."

"Let's give a try, then. You hold him still, and I'll do a test patch here around his left nipple."

Right up until the moment he felt the kiss of the torch, and smelled the unmistakable stench of burning hair, Claire knew her father didn't believe that either one of them actually had the guts to go through with it. From her position behind him, she couldn't see his facial expressions, but if his thrashing, struggling and moaning were any measure, she suspected he was now a confirmed believer in the strength of their convictions.

The whole procedure ended up taking under a minute, and there were more than a couple of "shits" and "oh, fucks." But when Olivia stepped back to admire her handiwork, she seemed pleased with the results.

"Take a look, Claire. What do think?"

"Well, my first impression is that the stench is pretty awful, so you might want to try some alternate form of deforestation next time. But other than that, it looks like you did a pretty fair job. That nipple's got a nice second-degree burn going on it; but from the areola outward, it looks like nothing more serious than a day at the beach without sunscreen."

"You really think the stench is that bad?"

"Don't you?"

"Not really. I mean, sure, it's no rose garden. But it's not a deal breaker. And, besides, I'm willing to put up with a little personal discomfort in the name of science. Not to mention being able to get rid of that disgusting fur ASAP."

"Well, okay, if you feel that strongly about it, fire away."

"MMMPHHHH! MMPPPHHHH!"

"I think he has something he'd like to add to the conversation."

"He never gave a shit about listening to what we had to say...."

"True."

"MMMMMMMMMMPPPHHH!"

"Oh all right, I'll take the tape off for a second, but this better not be anymore of your trash-talking bullshit. I already told you, I'm bored with it."

Valentin shook his head no so Olivia picked a corner of the tape up and pulled it away enough to allow him to talk.

"Don't. Please. No more."

"I quote, Boo Hoo. Wah. Wah. Wah." She started to smooth the tape back into place."

"No. Please. I...I can make it worth your while."

"What?" Claire asked.

"I have cash...money...gold...lots of it... and it's all yours if you just let me go."

CHAPTER TWENTY-TWO

"He's lying," Claire said. "He's a fucking crybaby coward who'll say or do anything to save his ass."

"Well, there's no question he's a slimy, lying sack of shit. But in this particular instance, he happens to be telling the truth."

"You mean he really *has* money?"

"Yeah. From what I can tell, probably a ton of it. And like he said, it's in cash, or gold or something else completely portable and untraceable."

"How? Why? From where?"

"Tell her, fuck nuts. Tell her where her inheritance is going to come from."

He hesitated, and Olivia lowered the torch towards his crotch, her finger caressing the ignition button.

"The website. Membership fees from Dr. Lollipuss.com."

"And?"

"Merchandise. Photo sets. Videos. DVD's. Audio tapes."

"Olivia, how much money is he talking about here?"

"A shit load of it. Tax free and squirreled away over a lot of years. More than likely, he's got millions."

"Millions? Millions? You made *millions* selling pictures of you sexually abusing me and Olivia and Tandy and who knows how many others, on the fucking Internet?" she screamed. Her right hand shot up and she dug her fingers dug into the soft flesh of his neck on either side of his Adams apple.

"Give me that thing," she said, snatching the torch from Olivia's hand. "I'm going to melt your cock and balls into S'mores." She let go of his neck and reached down, grabbed the end of his rapidly retreating penis and stretched it forward like a tube of Silly Putty.

"*No! No!* Get this crazy bitch away from me or you'll never find a dime of that money."

"Newsflash, asshole, I don't give a flying fuck about money," she said, punching the ignition switch.

"*Put it down, Claire!*"

"Olivia?" Claire looked up and found herself staring down the barrel of her father's gun. She dropped both the torch and the penis and backed up a step. "Olivia, what are you doing?"

"You might not give a fuck about the money, Claire, but I do. It's what I came here for, and I'm not leaving without it."

"Money. After all that's happened, to both of us, you're making this about money?"

"Yeah, pretty much. The money, getting Tandy away from this asshole permanently, fucking with both you and your Big Daddy there, all items on today's to-do list."

"So you really did help plan this...you weren't just playing along with Tandy when you showed up this morning?"

"Shit, I hope you catch on quicker than that on the job, or you're going to single-handedly turn the city of Albany into the Land of the Fucking Dead. And I wouldn't use the word "plan," exactly. It was more an engineering exercise...you know, a little phone call here, a whisper in the right little birdie's ear there, a little information, a little research, a little acting, a little pseudo-survivor-girl-bonding. And when it all comes together, Tandy and I will be walk away from this shit-hole town and find a place so far away we can forget any of you ever existed...you know, just like you did when you blew out of town."

"Olivia..."

"Enough talk, Claire. Take that roll of duct tape, plant yourself in the wheelchair and tape down your legs for me."

"Olivia, you don't have to do this."

"Yeah, I do. It's on the list." She screwed her features up into her old Crazy Lady face and held up an imaginary piece of paper. "See, item number three, have Claire tape herself to wheelchair." She grinned. "Nah...I'm just fucking with you." She stalked up to Valentin and shook the invisible document in his face. "It's really number five, right after doing something really nasty to Big Daddy here if he doesn't tell me where *the fucking money is!*"

"Eat shit you demented bitch! Go ahead and burn me if you've got the balls. It doesn't matter; I know you crazy cunts are never going to let me walk out of here, no matter what I say. Toast me into a fucking crispy critter if you want, but I ain't telling you shit."

"What did I tell you before about boring me with your bullshit?" Olivia slapped the tape back over his mouth, but as she walked toward Claire, she was smiling. She grabbed the roll out of Claire's hands and after trussing her legs up, Olivia tucked the pistol back into her pants and finished by duct taping Claire's wrists together again.

"Sorry about the gun. I really hate using it, but sometimes you have to take the traditional route to get your point across. Personally though, I prefer more creative methods of persuasion."

Olivia unlocked the brakes on Claire's chair and wheeled her over so that she was sitting right in front of her father again.

"Claire, I think you'll appreciate this, too, so I'm going to make sure you have a ringside seat. Now, give me a couple of min- utes, I've got to get a few things set up, and then we'll get started."

Claire and her father stared at each other silently while Olivia flitted around the room, ducking in and out of the kitchen, pulling a few things out of Tandy's duffel bags, finally retrieving something wrapped in a cocoon of blankets from outside and setting it down on the coffee table.

"Okay, I think I've got everything. Claire, let's begin with a question...you lived with your father for almost eighteen years. In all those years, can you remember him ever being afraid of anyone?"

"No."

"Can you remember him ever being afraid of any *thing*?"

"No...oh yeah...I remember he hated bugs...cockroaches mostly, I think. Something about having one get stuck in his ear when he lived in an apartment in Hartford after he got back from Korea."

"Good...good to know Tandy can tell the truth from time to time. This would have been *so* embarrassing if the cockroach story was just one of her little fibs." Olivia picked up the blanket-wrapped object and carefully unwrapped a gallon-sized clear glass bottle, half-filled with squirming, seething cockroaches.

Olivia held the jar close to her body, and the insects, energized by her body heat, increased their scuttling. She walked over to Valentin and held them out for him to see. He jerked away like she had hit him with the torch again. "The poor little guys are cold. I wasn't planning on leaving them outside so long. But, don't worry, we're going to warm them up soon enough."

She put the jar back on the coffee table and turned to her audience, like a teacher preparing to deliver an important lecture to a less-than-attentive class.

"Did either of you know that cockroaches can swim? It's true. They can even live submerged in water for up to forty minutes. They're also omnivores, so they'll eat just about anything, including human flesh, if it's all they can find. " She paused to let that tidbit of information sink in.

"But...enough of this Animal Planet shit. What all of this really comes down to is, Valentin, I want you to tell me where that money is and I'm going to give you until I finish assembling this little science project of mine to tell me. Claire, I want you to help keep time by singing that little Do-do-do game show song. You know the one where they only have something like sixty seconds to answer the final question. Start now please."

"Uh..do-do-do, da do-do, doot da doo do do..."

"Good. Keep that up."

Claire do-do'd while Olivia put on a pair of rubber gloves, took off the top of the roach jar and poured in the large pitcher of water she had brought in from the kitchen. When the jar was filled to the top, she quickly screwed on a new lid, one that sported a long, thick, clear plastic garden hose arching out of the top of it. The hose was about six feet long; and about a foot from the jar end, an enormous hemostat pinched the inch wide hose shut.

On the other end, Olivia attached an inflatable, double-ballooned, retention enema nozzle from Tandy's magic bag.

"Doot doot doot."

"Okay time's up! Shit, where's that damn plant hanger, I had it just a second ago...oh, here it is." Olivia expertly slipped the macramé support onto the jar, flipped it over so the tubing dangled down and hung it from the hook above Valentin's head. Finding that he was now face to face with the jar of madly paddling roaches, Valentin's moans turned to muffled screams and his eyes rolled around in his sockets so violently Claire was convinced they'd pop out and roll across floor like squishy marbles.

"Only one thing left to do," Olivia said, waggling the pumpkin- shaped nozzle in front of him.

"MMMMPPPPHHH! MMMMMPPHPHHH!"

"You'd better not be wasting my time. If we're going to go through with this, I want those roaches nice and lively."

Valentin whipped his head back and forth. Olivia nodded and ripped the tape off.

"The swamp. The money's in the swamp. Plastic bags, big plastic bags, weighed down with the gold bars, hanging in the water from the chains along the bateau bridge."

"Very creative, but why should I believe you?"

"Because, it's the truth. They're there. Claire knows where they are. I set one of the chains up with body parts once just to scare her. The ones with the money are in the same place."

"Well, you sound earnest enough, but we've already established you're a lying sack of shit. So I think the smart way to handle this is to go ahead, insert this bad boy, and get these roaches rolling into their new home.

"If you're telling the truth, when we come back, I'll pull it out...but if you're lying and you send me on a wild goose chase... not only will I leave your new friends where they are, I'll bring in the other jar of roaches and a nice, thick feeding tube."

CHAPTER TWENTY-THREE

Claire sat in the chair, mesmerized. It was like watching the bad reality shows she called car wreck television. The scene playing out in front of her was horrifying, but she couldn't bring herself to look away.

Growing up, enemas had been her father's second favorite way to make her take her medicine. She had spent a lot of time bent over with a hose up her ass, but it was nothing like the tableau Olivia had set up here.

Granted, Olivia was probably psychotic, and obviously dangerous; but she still couldn't help admitting to a sneaking admiration for the woman's panache. It was all she could do not to cheer when, after her father failed to obey Olivia's order to stop squirming, she pulled out the gun and jammed it between his ass cheeks. She then asked him sweetly to choose which one he would rather have go off up there.

From that point on, the rest of the insertion procedure went smoothly. She was able to get the wide, ridged nozzle implanted and properly inflated without any further protests. After a final yank on the thick, silicon tubing locked in the rectal seal, Olivia released the clamp and the roaches started their southward journey.

Valentin wasn't in a position to see the hemostats being unclamped, but there was no mistaking the loud, metallic *snick* sound that echoed in the quiet room. Olivia and Claire watched in fascination as the bugs bumped and surged their way down the tube, propelled by the rushing water. It only took seconds for the first vanguard to surf their way through the piping and disappear into Valentin's body.

"You bitch! You crazy cunt! I told you where the money is. Get them out! Get them out of me! Oh God, I can feel them...I can feel

them inside of me!"

"Not a lot of fun to have uninvited company in there is it, Big Daddy?" Olivia asked before turning her attention to Claire. "All right, it looks like everything's under control here. Let's head down to the swamp and see if your Daddy is telling the truth or not."

Olivia cut Claire's hands and legs free of the tape and pulled her to her feet.

"We're going to walk down to the swamp, nice and easy. I really don't want to shoot you, but I won't hesitate if you try to run, or fight, or get between me and that money. Understood?"

Claire nodded yes, but knew neither her brain or her heart understood anything about this situation. Rage, justice, revenge -those motivations she got, but greed was just something that didn't track for her. She wasn't naïve-- she knew there were people who would kill you for the change in your pocket-- but it was hard to imagine the Olivia she had known as being one of them.

"All right, let's go," Olivia ordered, giving her a shove toward the Lodge's front door.

* * * *

Claire didn't know what she was expecting, but it wasn't the blindingly bright sunshine that greeted them as they walked out of the Lodge and started toward the swamp. "What time is it?" she asked Olivia.

"It's almost noon."

"Noon? Which day?"

"Wednesday, April 13th."

"Yesterday at this time, you and I were sitting down to a plateful of Lenny's banana chocolate chip griddle cakes and I was letting you sell me on this whole bullshit scheme. Goddammit, I'm an idiot."

"No, not an idiot, just a do-gooder. The major difference between the two is that do-gooders are way easier to manipulate. Just mention that some stranger is hurt or in danger of being hurt, and you throw yourselves 100% into the situation, no questions asked."

"How can you be so fucking cold-blooded? Do you know what your sister and my father did to me in there...what am I saying, of course you do. You *engineered* this. How could you do this to me?"

"The same way you left me here with that bastard and Tandy and all their shit, and then disappeared off the face of the planet without even a note to let me know my best friend was still alive."

"So this is payback?

"Partly. But, like I said before, this is mostly about the money. Fucking with you and your father is pure gravy."

"You hate me that much?"

"Nope, actually I don't hate you at all. Don't forget: the opposite of love isn't hate, baby, it's apathy. It took me a long time to work through it, but, to paraphrase Clooney's character in *From Dusk Till Dawn*: The rest of the world can live forever or die this second for all I care. The only things I give a shit about are me, that bitch in the kitchen, and our money."

The women lapsed into silence as the path curved away from the more heavily traveled parts of the Camp and deteriorated from carefully groomed crushed rock to a hard-packed dirt, then petered out to little more than an indentation in the grass that looked like a abandoned animal track. They followed the trail single-file around the lip of the small retention pond and veered off to the right, just before crossing into the electric company's property on the Camp's western edge.

Claire knew she should be trying to formulate some kind of escape plan as she plodded along, but her brain was frozen into a block of grey ice. Too much had happened over the last 24 hours, and it felt like all she could do to just put one foot in front of the other. She was glad she still had her sneakers and socks, but Tandy's over shirt wasn't much help keeping her warm against the April bluster. *Snap out of it or you'll die here*, the lizard bellowed at her.

Trying to get her mind off the forty degree temperature and the cold fingers of wind snapping against her normally covered body parts, Claire lifted her head and tried to take stock of her surround- ings. She had walked these paths every day of her child-hood, and was surprised at how little this part of the Fish Camp had changed. Despite how much the neighborhood surrounding the Camp had built up while she was gone, once they left the main buildings behind, this area was just as isolated, desolated and creepy as she remembered it. She could scream her head off out here and no one would ever hear her. In fact, the only people she had ever seen out this way, besides the odd trespassing hunter or group of stoners looking for a place to party, were electric company employees bouncing along the access road as they came and went on their monthly equipment inspections.

Claire scanned the narrow sea of tall grass and shrubs near the road and the woods that rose up along the perimeter, searching for some sign of life besides her and Olivia, but knew the chances were slim to none. An orange vest, smoke from a campfire, even the sound of a distant rifle shot would be music to her ears about now. Briefly, she caught a flash of something shiny off to her left, but it was gone before she could figure out if it was manmade or just the sunlight bouncing off one of the mica-covered boulders that littered the ground. She didn't see it again, and within a few yards, they turned north into the woods that ringed the swamp.

"Be careful where you're walking," Olivia warned as they started the steep descent. "April showers still bring quick mud around here."

Quick mud. Now there was a disgusting blast from the past. The stuff was thicker and more viscous than quicksand, and slimier and smellier than regular mud. It never sucked anyone under completely, but it was easy to sink knee or even hip-deep in it and not be able to get out on your own. She had lost track of the number of times she'd been trapped in it as a kid and had to scream for someone to come and pull her out.

"Look, there's the old shack," Olivia said, pointing to a roughly rectangular pile of boards and tar paper that somehow still clung precariously to the hill, its back half-jutting out into the space above the quagmire. "Remember how we used to call it the pimple on the ass of the swamp? It's hard to believe God hasn't popped that thing by now."

Panic clawed at Claire's throat as they picked their way

down the last thirty feet of trail leading to the bateau bridge. The stench of wet, moldering decay crawled up her nostrils. Flashes of memory from her last visit here flickered through her head like a stereoscopic slide show. As they rounded the last stand of evergreens, the swamp spread out in front of them, rotted trees poking up through the black water like broken teeth in a corpse's mouth.

Claire froze, her gaze fixated on the wood and pontoon contraption that floated in front of them.

"I can't," she said as Olivia prodded her forward.

"Don't tell me the big heroic paramedic is afwaid of a widdle bit of dirty water?"

"You know damn well..."

"Yep, know but don't care. If your father is telling the truth, large stacks of bills are heavy. Add gold to it, and it's going to take muscle to get that money up out of the water and back to the car. So get moving, or I'll put a bullet in your gut, throw you in, and wait to see what kills you first: blood loss, fear, or whatever else lives down in there. Muuuwwwahhhhhhh."

"Sick...Olivia, you're sick."

"Already established. And the only cure costs lots and lots of *mon-ey*, so haul ass or go swimming."

Claire shuffled forward and stepped gingerly up onto the first of the floating boards. The bridge was made of old, weather-worn planks laid across a series of empty, lashed-together, 55-gallon oil drums stretched out from one bank of the swamp to the other. There were no safety rope or railings; and since the bridge bounced and rolled with every movement, walking across it required a lot more grace and balance than Claire was normally capable of.

"C'mon," Olivia ordered, poking her in the back with the gun.

One foot at a time. Left. Right. Claire kept her eyes down and stared at her feet, willing them to move and trying not to think about the dark, scummy water that lapped and splashed over the boards with every step.

"Okay, halt. There's the first chain over there on the right.

Kneel down and pull it up."

Claire slowly lowered her body to her hands and knees and crawled over to the edge. She grabbed the thick cable and pulled. Whatever was down there was heavy, and it seemed to fight her as she inched it above the surface. She could taste the bile in her mouth as her stomach twisted and churned.

At first she didn't see anything beyond the metal links; but slowly, a shadow appeared through the murk, growing larger the closer she pulled it. Giving a final heave, the object broke through the surface. It took a minute or two of frantic pawing, but eventually she was able to snag the slippery plastic sack and drag it onto the bridge.

It was one of those heavy-duty, vacuumed sealed storage bags, and it was filled with bundles of cash and what looked like several flat rectangles of gold.

CHAPTER TWENTY-FOUR

"I'll be damned, the bastard was telling the truth!" Olivia said, kneeling down beside Claire and wiping away the scum to get a better look inside the bag. "I know you don't give a shit about money, but come on, even you have to be impressed by this."

"I...I can't believe it. I knew drug dealers had this kind of money, but I never thought...this...from a bunch of pictures."

"Supply and demand. Porn is big business...child porn, to the right buyer, is unfortunately damn close to priceless. All right, we need to pull up the rest of the bags and hump it out at least to the main trail. If I have to, I'll get the ATV out of the boathouse and move them to the van that way."

Olivia got to her feet and leveled the gun at Claire's head. "I'm going to take a quick count and see how many bags we're dealing with here. Sit tight, and don't make me prove I can still shoot the nipple off a rat's tit at twenty yards."

Claire watched her walk the length of the bridge, stopping every so often to lean over and look at what she assumed were more chains hanging into the water. *Jump,* the lizard whispered, *it's your only chance.* No. *Jump or you'll die.* Not a chance. There are worse things than dying and most of them are right here in this swamp. *How can it be worse than what they've already done to you? Jump!* She didn't want to. She knew that right below the surface some combination of cold dead hands and writhing tentacles and gnashing teeth were waiting to tear her apart. *If you die, Olivia and Tandy win. She's turning. Go! Go NOW!*

She didn't mind dying, but the thought of them winning enraged her. She didn't jump, but she did move. She knew any large, sudden motions would instantly be telegraphed across the bridge so she bent forward, sucked down a deep lungful of air and slipped quietly into the cold, fetid water.

Claire knew she only had a few seconds before the pontoon's bounce back would give her away and Olivia would start shooting. She needed to get out of range, go deep or go wide, or both. She forced her eyes open and tried to get her bearings, but anything more than an inch or two away was a wall of muddy shadows. A flash of metal plowing down from above and something brushing up against her ankle from below sent her bolting in a blind panic. She began to swim. She didn't know where she was going; she just had to get away.

The water was thick and dark and claustrophobic. Submerged trees, assorted woodland debris and rusting metal hulks of various sizes and shapes appeared out of the gloom like pop-up scares on a haunted amusement park ride. She tried to swim away from where Olivia was aiming, but it was impossible to tell direction when she couldn't see more than a couple of inches in front of her face.

Her lungs began to burn as the seconds ticked on. She had to get to the surface and grab a breath but she knew that's what Olivia was waiting for. Ahead on her right there was something fairly large and solid near the water line, maybe a fallen tree she could use for cover, so she swam for it. It wasn't until she was within inches of the surface that she realized where she was. She had got- ten completely turned around and was coming back up underneath the bridge...and Olivia.

If there was any other option, she would have taken it, but she didn't have the oxygen to go any farther. She aimed for the space between two of the 55-gallon drums and rose slowly through the water, trying to make as little noise and as few ripples as possible. As she surfaced, Claire grabbed onto the lip of the floating barrel and sucked in the air greedily, letting her feet tread water beneath her. Six inches above her head, Olivia's footsteps pounded on the wooden boards as she stalked back and forth looking for some sign of her.

"Claire! Oh Claire! Come out, come out, wherever you are!" Olivia called. "You know you can't get away. There's no way out and nowhere you can hide." More footsteps, but at least no more gunshots.

"You better have drowned, bitch, cause if I have to hunt your ass down, I'm handing it over to Tandy to play with... and you know how destructive she can be with her toys."

Another pass across the bridge, slower, not so frantic.

"The water's still cold here in April. If you're out there, I bet you're getting really chilly by now. I bet if I listened real hard, I could hear your teeth chattering."

Olivia paused for a minute. "Nope, nothing yet. But don't worry, the hypothermia will be setting in soon. And once you start shivering, I'll just follow the ripples until I find you."

Claire hated to admit it, but Olivia was right. She could feel the cold seeping into her hands and feet. It was getting harder and harder to hold onto the thin edge of the oil drum or feel if her feet were still moving.

Footsteps back and forth, back and forth, softer to louder to softer as Olivia paced out her death watch above her head. Claire began to shiver. She pulled her knees up to her chest and tried to curl into a ball, but it didn't stop the cold water from pressing in on her skin, trying to steal her breath and freeze her heartbeat. Her teeth chattered, and she ducked deeper into the water to mute the sound.

Claire could feel her mind slipping sideways as icy fingers began to crawl through her central nervous system and up into her brain. She needed to get out of here, but there was some reason she wasn't supposed to. Minutes ticked by as she tried to remember, but it was too much effort. She was so cold...cold and tired. If she could just close her eyes for a second...

She felt her exhaustion wrap around her like a thick quilt and, as she gave into it, her hands dropped away from the barrel and she slipped below the surface.

Claire! Claire, wake up NOW!

Her eyes snapped open. Sunlight filtered down through the yards of water above her head, brightening the area around her. She was planted ankle deep in the muck of the swamp floor while an underwater forest of human corpses bobbed and swayed around her. There were dozens of them. They surrounded her, crowding in close and filling her vision. Some were nothing more than skeletons festooned in tattered remnants of clothing, while others were a CSI slideshow of the stages of body decomposition. All were tethered in place by chains that wrapped around their bodies and disappeared into mud below their feet.

She turned and felt them bump against her. Their decayed arms and skeletal hands moved with and toward her, reaching out to her, pleading with her to join them. Her chest burned. She fought the urge to open her mouth and scream. Instead, she gathered all the strength left in her body and launched herself up through the filthy soup. Gasping and coughing, she broke through the algae covered surface and threw herself toward the nearest arm of dry land, the raised pyre of a beaver dam.

Hand over hand, Claire dragged herself up and across the collection of sticks, mud and moss until she was completely out of the water. She lay there for what seemed like forever, shivering and gulping air until her heart stopped pounding and her brain began to sluggishly reengage. What the hell had happened down there? The bodies couldn't have been real, could they? It must have been some sort of near death hallucination...

The distant whining of a small engine finished pulling her out of her stupor. *Olivia! Shit, she's got the ATV, and she's on her way back for the money.*

She had to get out of here now. She pushed herself to a sitting position and began the arduous task of picking her way back onto dry land. Thankfully her sneakers were still intact, but Tandy's shirt had been reduced to little more than a shredded dishrag. She needed to get her hands on some warm, dry clothing and a weapon if she was going to have any chance of making it out of here alive.

The closest building to the swamp, not counting the shack, was her father's house. As much as she hated the idea of going back there, at the moment, it was her best bet. She didn't care if she had to break in. He and Tandy were safely tucked away at the Lodge and Olivia would be busy down here loading the money up.

CHAPTER TWENTY-FIVE

Spurred on by the increasing drone of the ATV, Claire stayed low and scrambled up the wooded slope as fast as she could. Her goal was the stand of evergreens at the ridgeline. Once she got beyond them, she'd be invisible to anyone anywhere on that side of the swamp, and she could continue back to the Camp without worrying about being seen.

It was close, but she made it to the top and ducked under the thick, feathery pine boughs just as Olivia nosed the ATV around the final curve of the path. Claire watched as Olivia parked the machine, took out her gun and carefully circled the edge of the swamp, presumably making one last sweep looking for her. When she didn't find anything, she put the gun back in her waistband and got down to the business of plundering the bateau. Claire shook her head as she watched. It was hard for her to process that Olivia was really going to go through with this. She was really going to steal *this money* and use it to finance a brand new life with Tandy. Claire felt the wave of rage wash through her body. It was all she could do not to run back down there and throw herself at Olivia, gun be damned. But she had to be smart about this.

She would not, could not, allow Olivia and Tandy to walk away from this. Olivia had pushed so hard for her to admit to the existence of her inner monster. Well, now she and her batshit sister could just deal with her up close and personal.

All of her life, Claire had run away from her biology, her genetics and her early training. Every day she had battled for control over her basic nature in order to pass as a decent, productive member of human society, and look where it had gotten her. She had wasted all those years following the rules instead of her instincts, and society's laws instead of her own sense of justice.

Aurelio's favorite curse, *Basta! Enough!* screamed inside her head, and the reptilian monster roared to life.

She would stop Olivia and Tandy, but now was not the time. Even with the help of the ATV, Claire estimated it would take Olivia at least an hour or two to complete her thievery and go back to the Lodge for Tandy. It wasn't a lot of time, but it would have to be enough.

She left the tree line and started back toward the camp. The old trails were right were she remembered them, and she was able to follow them all the way to the clump of Mountain Laurel bushes that lined the path in front of her father's house. Carefully, she pushed her way through the tightly packed branches and scanned the property for signs of activity. Given that Tandy, Olivia and her father were all accounted for, she wasn't quite sure who she expected to pop out at her. But considering the way the last 24 hours had gone, it seemed smart to play it careful.

After making sure all was as quiet as it should be, Claire broke cover and circled around to the back of the house looking for an easy way inside. She wasn't exactly surprised to see that very little had changed from the way she remembered it as a child. Firewood was still stacked precisely under a neatly folded and tied down tarp, garden tools were all locked away in their shed, the patio was swept clean ...and the hatchway doors were standing wide open.

There was no way in hell her father had left the basement open like this. *Olivia.* It had to be. She had said she found those pictures, along with other evidence of his kiddy porn empire, in a secret place somewhere in the basement. So, the lying bitch managed to tell the truth about something, anyway. Still, there was an off chance she also could have left some sort of trap set up, so it wouldn't hurt to be on her guard.

She moved closer to the doors and then stopped and listened. Silence. After years of playing Movie Quote War with Jim, her mind immediately jumped to her favorite lines from *The Silence of the Lambs.* "Our Billy wasn't born a criminal, Clarice. He was made one through years of systematic abuse." Amen to that, Brother Hannibal.

"Aurelio, what I wouldn't give to have your skinny butt backing me up right about now," she said under her breath. It could be a trap she supposed, but a cold gust of wind fluttering through the remnants of Tandy's shirt reminded her that she wasn't exactly dripping in options at the moment. So she took a deep breath and started down the cement steps.

She had hoped to find some old clothes, an old pair of overalls or gardening clothes, maybe even a box of her own stuff that she had left behind, but it didn't take long for her to realize there was nothing like that down here. She did find the remnants of the false wall and shelves that Olivia had mentioned, but other than that and the usual household machinery – water pump, furnace, oil tank and ancient family freezer he used to store fish and game meat – the rest of the room was barren. She wasn't thrilled about it, but it looked like she was going to have to go into his room if she wanted to find anything to wear...or something to kill him with.

As for weapons: when she was a kid, he had kept a collection of hunting rifles and shot guns locked away in the gun cabinet in his den. But there had been another gun, a handgun, and it wasn't the one he had in the recliner. This one had been old, a revolver with an elaborately carved wooden handle that he had kept hidden in the right boot of a pair of fishing waders hanging at the back of his closet. She had found it one day when he was being especially violent and she was trying to literally disappear into the woodwork. She still remembered how the gun felt the first time she touched it. It had been that same stomach-dropping feeling she got when she looked down from one of the high branches of the cherry tree in the side yard. It was terrifying and exciting at the same time. The metal had been ice cold, but the thick grips with the beautiful flying horse carved in it felt warm and friendly somehow. After that first day, she snuck back to it as often as she could. She lost hours running her fingers over and over along the ridges and furrows that formed that design.

Claire hadn't thought about that wooden carving in years, but when she looked down at her hand, her fingers were tracing the outline of the horse into the cold flesh of her thigh. It had been her own private little good luck symbol, something she had drawn over and over whenever she was nervous or scared. The horse had helped keep her strong and safe. She let her fingers continue their work as she climbed the wooden slat stairs to the main floor of the house.

The door at the top was closed, but it opened easily when she pushed it. She paused to listen, but was very aware of the minutes ticking by. If she wanted to ambush Olivia, she was going to have to get over to the Lodge and be ready when she came back to pick up Tandy...and deliver whatever coup de grace she had planned for her father.

Claire knew Olivia would never leave her father alive. She hated him too much, and Tandy loved him too much. If he was alive, or if Tandy even *thought* he was alive, she would move heaven and earth to get back to him. The only way Olivia had a chance of saving Tandy was if she killed him in front of her. Claire planned to be at the Lodge before that happened. But would it be to stop her, or just to make sure the bastard was actually dead?

Claire's eyes strayed down the hall toward the closed door to her old bedroom. How many nights had she laid there as a little girl, her eyes wide with fear, praying that her father's footsteps didn't stop outside her door? Praying that she didn't hear the string of bells she had hung on the back of her doorknob jingle as he turned it? Praying that just for tonight there was no medicine to take before she could go to sleep?

The memories of the fear and pain flooded back, but this time, instead of being sucked under, she felt herself surfing along the top of them, using their power and momentum to move her forward. No, she wouldn't stop Olivia from killing her father if she got to him first, but that wouldn't be the end of it. Not only would she make sure that he was most sincerely dead, but she'd also make damn sure his little psychopathic dog Tandy and her cunt of a sister followed him to Hell.

When she was little, she had believed if she could just be good enough and quiet enough and obedient enough, God would answer her prayers and save her. He would reach down from his golden throne, lift her onto his shoulders and piggyback her to a place where no one would ever hurt her again. But God never came. Eventually, she stopped waiting to be rescued and became the rescuer.

And now, as she thought about Olivia, Tandy, and her father, she realized it was time to stop waiting for God to act and take matters into her own hands.

She walked past her bedroom and down the hall to the master bedroom. Throughout her entire childhood, or at least from the day her mother disappeared on, this room had always been strictly a man's space. No flowers, no frills, no ornamentation. Dark colors, simple, functional furnishings and above all, everything kept neat and squared away. When Claire opened the door, she had to close her eyes and open them again to make sure she wasn't having a seizure of some kind.

As she looked around the room, the first image that flashed through her mind was that a circus full of clowns had vomited up the 120 count crayon boxes all over the walls... and then exploded. Her head swam as she tried to take in the visual chaos: a multicolored pile of panties falling out of a dresser drawer, a cerulean lamp shade, fuchsia pillow cases, teal sheets, lime green curtains, and a pair of burnt sienna boots sitting in the middle of the room. Tandy. At least she was consistent. Claire imagined this a pretty fair representation of the rat's nest that was Tandy's brain.

Claire turned to the closet and hoped that that, at least, had escaped Tandy-ization. But if anything, the smaller space was worse. Tightly packed clothes, most still with the price and security tags still attached bowed the thick metal rod. More stacks of brightly colored clothes towered above her on shelves, and piles of shoes and boots were piled three and four deep covering every inch of floor space. Claire didn't know if she could even fight her way to the spot in the back where she had last seen her father's waders. Were any of her father's clothes even in here any more, or had he given it all over to Tandy's five-finger discount collection?

"I don't have time for this shit," Claire said, looking at the mess. The first time she had found the gun she had been crawling around the back of the closet, so she dropped to her knees and waded in. As she fought her way through the mess, she remembered why she had chosen this particular closet that day. Her third grade teacher had read just finished reading them C.S. Lewis' *The Lion, the Witch and the Wardrobe* and she had been looking for a secret door. It hadn't mattered if the door led to another part of the house, or another world. She had just been hoping for a way out.

She hadn't found a door; but when she turned to come back out, she had seen what looked like a man standing there behind her father's clothes. She could see his boots and his pant legs disappearing up into the dark above her head. She had clamped her hand over her mouth, but she had screamed a little anyway. She froze, waiting for him to reach out and grab her. But as her eyes adjusted to the dark, she realized what was terrifying her was a pair of father's fishing pants.

It had been just about here, she thought reaching the back wall. She turned and started pawing through the hanging cloth until she spotted them, crammed into the deepest corner. She yanked the waders down off their hook and dragged them out of the closet like a dog dragging home a deer carcass. She felt the uneven weight, and her heart soared as she reached down into the right leg and came up with not only the heavy firearm, but a box of ammunition as well.

Claire never guessed that it would actually take longer for her to find a pair of pants and shirt of Tandy's that didn't glow in the dark than it took her to find her father's gun. Luckily, size wasn't a problem – she and Tandy were a perfect match – but the girl didn't own one piece of clothing that could even be described as neutral. Finally, she climbed into a pair of eggplant colored jeans, stole a sweatshirt from her father's drawers, loaded the guns and ammo in the pockets, and took off for The Lodge.

CHAPTER TWENTY-SIX

Claire was a little more than half way through the small strip of woods that separated her father's house from the Lodge when she caught sight of the white van parked near the building's back door. Shit, it had to be Olivia. She'd beaten her back there.

She dug the gun out of her sweatshirt and held it down at her side as she warily circled the vehicle, staying low. The van was sitting half on and half off the gravel path, with its nose pointed out toward the parking lot and one of its rear doors ajar. All appeared quiet, but Claire knew if the van was here, so was Olivia. There was no way in hell that greedy bitch would let that money out of her sight.

Claire crept closer. The front seats were empty. She said a quick prayer that the keys were at least in the ignition. No such luck, so she eased around to the back. Holding the gun with one hand, she pushed her way through the open rear door with the other.

The cargo space was crammed floor to ceiling with, not just the bags of money, but with stacks of boxes, piles of computers and equipment and loads of what looked like bookkeeping and business files.

What the hell was Olivia up to? She said her father ran a kiddy porn business, and that there were CD's, DVD's, tapes and photos. But what was she planning on doing with them?

Claire pulled open one of the boxes closest to her and quickly rifled through the contents. Holy shit, there were names. And hundreds of them. Names, street addresses, IPO addresses, credit card numbers, the works.

She was looking at the contact and financial information for every pervert who had ever logged into Dr. Lollipuss.com.

She dug deeper into the box and found a file her father had

titled "Heavy Hitters". She flipped it open and found another, shorter list of names that included detailed notes about each one of these special snowflakes, including their preferences, the amount of time and money they could be counted on to blow every month, and if they produced and shared their own amateur work or not.

She shoved the box back into the van and left the door hanging. This could be big. This could be huge. So much bigger than her father, Olivia and Tandy. So much bigger than anything she'd ever dreamed of. Her mind spun with the possibilities of the epic damage she could cause these assholes. She could destroy careers, reputations, even lives with this kind of evidence.

It was, without question, the right thing to do. *Just hop in the van, drive off right now, and spend the rest of your life...*

"AAAHHHHHHH!" The scream came from inside the Lodge. A woman's scream. Or was it two? Up and then gone, like coyote kill-shrieks in the night.

"*Fuck,*" she hissed, yanked back into the moment. Even as the word don't flashed through her mind, eighteen years of EMS training already had pushed her into motion.

But not for saving lives, this time. She needed closure. And for that, she needed those keys.

CHAPTER TWENTY-SEVEN

Claire ran to the side of the building, flattened herself against the wall and slid toward the back door. It, too, had been left half- open. Carefully, she moved forward, peeking through. All was clear in the immediate area. But muffled voices and banging sounds were coming from the direction of the main room.

Claire slipped inside and tiptoed down the hall, stepping over the remnants of the shattered pantry door. And the biggest butcher knife was now missing from the block. Outstanding. Fuck squared.

That might explain the screaming.

Cautiously, she approached the swinging door between the kitchen and the main room. The noises were louder now. Claire could clearly hear Tandy's voice, and the slap of skin on skin.

"*BENJAMIN! BENJAMIN!* Answer me!" Slap. Slap. "*Benjamin!*"

Claire held her breath. Was he already dead? Had Olivia and her cockroaches really killed him? "Don't you dare be dead yet, you son of a bitch," she muttered under her breath.

Then she heard a cough and a sputter that turned to a long, undulating, keening banshee's wail.

"*OH, GOD! OH, GOD! GET THEM OUT OF ME! GET IT OUT OF ME...!*"

"What, Daddy? The tube?"

"Yes, the tube, you fuckwit! *I CAN FEEL THEM CRAWLING INSIDE ME!*"

"Okay! Okay! Shhhh... hold still, while...AAAUGH!!!"

Claire pushed through the door and craned her neck around the corner in time to see Tandy jerk the tube free, unleashing a torrent of shit, water and roaches that exploded out of his body and rained down on the floor some fifteen feet away. Claire would have bet that the little buggers had drowned by now; but from Tandy's frantic La Cucaracha dance, it looked like some of them were proving the species could survive anything.

"OH, GOD! COCKROACHES!" Tandy screamed as she stomped. "I can't fucking STAND roaches! They're SO fucking gross!"

"GAHHH!" he screamed in concert. "Goddamit, THEY'RE STILL EATING ME!"

If she'd been waiting for her moment, it was this.

"Step away from him," Claire said, moving into the room, her gun aimed straight at the back of Tandy's head. Tandy jumped at the sound, and Big Daddy looked up at her with a jolt of genuine confusion. He had never looked so fragile or frightened. Good.

"YOU PUT THAT GUN DOWN NOW!" he bellowed.

"Uh-uh," she said, stepping closer. Not putting down the gun.

Tandy turned, and Claire could see the blood all over her. Fresher blood than before, and a whole lot more.

"Claire!" Tandy said. "Wow, my bad. I thought Olivia killed your ass hours ago."

"Oh, she gave it her best shot," Claire said. "But face it. The batshit crazy tend to fall down on for the follow-through."

The pool table was between them, the wide way. So many implements of torture upon it. Tandy stepped toward it and picked up a red one. The knife in question.

"Put it down," Claire said.

"What, this?" Tandy's eyes sparkled hard as the blade. She moved away from Big Daddy, long way down the table. "You want this one?"

"Put it down before I blow a hole through your skull and let all the psycho drain out." Claire took a couple steps forward and sideways, pacing her, less than six feet away.

"I don't see it," Tandy laughed, kept going, coming up to the end, still waving the knife. "I see a liar."

"Would you just fucking kill her? GAAHHH!" Claire's father screamed.

"With her pants on fire."

"Tandy. Christ," Claire said, arms steady, never dropping her gaze or her aim from Tandy's eyes as both of them stepped around the end of the table.

Then Claire tripped over something large and wet, was already falling before she registered Olivia's dead eyes and hamburgered face: stabbed over and over, then left to bleed out by the corner pocket.

The air filled with Tandy's mad laughter, rushing forward as Claire hit the floor, rolled, and aimed upward, drawing a bead on the pearly white grin that suddenly froze above her, knife upraised and equally frozen.

"You don't have the fucking b--", Tandy said.

Claire just smiled, and pulled the trigger.

Tandy's teeth blew up through her skull, raining warm blood, bone shards, and brain jelly down in Claire's face like a summer hailstorm. It felt like baptism to her reptile self. Everything clarified, in that terrible moment.

Tandy buckled at the knees and dropped, but it seemed like slow motion, how long it took, just looking up at her falling, off to the side and landing on Olivia's corpse. Thumping face on breast, then lolling twisted. Two dead sisters, staring upward at nothing.

And then, at last, it was just Claire and Big Daddy.

Claire lay on the floor for a minute, staring up at the same ceiling Tandy and Olivia would have seen. Only she was seeing something. Letting the pieces fall together in her mind. Letting the clarity soak in. There was no hurry, all of a sudden. Time was no longer an issue.

In some faraway distance, her father shouted something. She couldn't tell what it was. She didn't care. She was beyond listening. It helped that her ears were still ringing from the .45's blast, and her shoulder throbbed from the kick of it. They were distractions, but they helped her focus. So did his voice.

"Okay," she said.

Claire sat up, wiped the mess from her face, wiped the mess from her gun, and stood.

You can do anything you want, said the reptile brain. *Nobody will hear him scream. Nobody hears anyone scream. That's why the screaming never stops.*

"I know," she said, and turned toward her father. He was strung up, just as they'd left him: naked and flaccid, helplessly writhing before her. Whatever "medicine" he had left between his legs was crawling back into his balls as he looked in her eye, and saw how done with him she was.

She wondered if that was how he felt, when he looked at all his victims: so beyond indifferent you couldn't wait to shut them up, yet so caught up in the moment you wanted to milk it for all it was worth.

Whatever the case, he shut up for a second as she walked toward him. His eyes were still defiant, but his lips were trembling like a little old man's. Like the little old man he had suddenly become.

Claire raised her gun and sighted down the barrel, aiming for the notch between his eyes. He quivered and moaned. A stream of urine ran down his leg, mixing with the shit and cockroach carcasses on the floor underneath him. She could feel the waves of terror rolling off of him, and it excited her. Damned if Olivia wasn't right. She was Daddy's little monster, after all.

"Claire," he said, as she shifted the barrel from his face to his crotch, back up just a little. Then he said something else that she didn't quite catch.

The .45 was way too loud.

Two point blank belly shots, one on either side of his spine, ripped through his intestines. Big Daddy shrieked in pain. Neither wound would kill him immediately, but by the time it was all over, he'd be singing Hallelujah to whatever dark god he worshipped, begging and praying for deliverance.

Whenever she and Jim played their Worst Ways to Die Game, gut shots always came out near the top. It was an excruciating way to go.

The only thing worse would be burning alive. Which, now that she mentioned it, was an excellent idea.

CHAPTER TWENTY-EIGHT

By the time she got to the boat house, found the gas cans, and schlepped them back inside the Lodge, she had run through all the details in her head and knew her plan was solid. Her car was in the lot. Zack would place her here last night. With Tandy as her stand- in, toothless and burnt beyond recognition, no one would have any reason to believe she was anything more than the victim of a brutal and senseless triple slaying.

It was too bad she couldn't say goodbye to Zack, hit Lenny's for one last celebratory breakfast. Too bad she couldn't go back to her apartment, to the life she'd built and the work she loved. Couldn't tell Jim what had happened. Couldn't tell anyone, ever.

A living Claire Valentin would spend the rest of her life in prison. There was no doubt about that. Even with all the evidence – even if some considered her a hero – any chance she had of genuine justice would be buried under the weight of her crime. She knew that the second she pulled the trigger. It was her moment of clarity, and she had accepted its consequences.

From that moment on, Claire was dead.

But the woman she had just become had no name, had no boundaries, and had several million dollars, not to mention a shit-load of priceless information. She had the keys to the van in her pocket. And a very clear vision of what must be done.

Back in the Lodge, it was time to say goodbye to everything that had come before.

"Good riddance," she said.

Claire uncapped the plastic containers and carefully emptied the gasoline over the bodies, saving her father for last. By the time she got to him, she was delighted to find that the roaches had swarmed from his open belly all the way to his face: pushing themselves up his nostrils, inside his ears, spilling into his mouth with every ragged breath.

"Oh, good," she said, as she gassed him up. "You're still alive. That has to suck."

"You suck my dick," he croaked. "You little whore." Remorseless, to the end.

Claire had to laugh. "Well, *that* ain't gonna happen. But thanks for going out on a high note, Dad. Nice to know that some things never change."

She set down the gas, knelt beside the pool table, picked up the *crème brulee* torch. He called her a couple of other choice names, through his mouthful of bugs, but they were all after the fact.

"You know what?" she said, as she lit the torch.

"Just die, you bastard. Die."

It took a while. She stuck around to make sure. But was gone long before the first sirens wailed, and the fire trucks rolled up to the ashes.

EPILOGUE

Claire had always loved autumn in Albany. The crisp air, the colorful leaves and that feeling of fresh beginnings left over from her school days. She was grateful that even though she didn't live here anymore, her business still afforded her the occasional opportunity to return to the place she would always think of as home.

She checked her GPS one last time; and when the friendly voice announced that she had arrived at her destination, she looked around and knew that she was in the right place. The little Taurus she drove now didn't have the style or power of her old LeBaron, but its one advantage was that it fit almost anywhere, even on an overcrowded street like Myrtle.

She got out of the car, smoothed out her nurse's scrubs, straightened her nametag and started up the impossibly long stone steps to the building's brightly painted second floor. She crossed the wide wood porch, stepped to the side of the door and rang the bell marked 863-Calvin.

A middle aged strawberry blonde woman answered the door. "Can I help you?"

"Hi," Claire said, showing her the laminated I.D. card she carried. "I'm Peg Bellerophon from Tri-City Rehabilitative Services. Mr. Calvin has an Physical Therapy appointment today."

"It's *Professor* Calvin. And I thought Estella came on Tuesdays."

"Estella called out sick," Claire said, leaning forward. "Female problems," she whispered.

"Oh. Well, I was just on my way out, but I guess could take you back and show you what he needs help with."

"That's okay, I'm sure Professor Calvin and I can figure it out."

"Momma! Momma! Let's go!" Claire smiled as the little blond girl bounced up to her mother and began dragging on her pant leg.

"You'll have to excuse Crista. She's very excited. I promised her she could help me pick out her birthday party decorations this afternoon."

"Well, that certainly qualifies as very urgent and important business that I wouldn't *dream* of keeping you from. By the way, Crista, how old are you going to be?"

"Saturday I'll be four years old and I'm going to have a party and cake and Uncle George said that since he's almost all better he'd make sure I had an extra special, super duper surprise!"

"Wow, Crista, that sounds wonderful! I hope you have the best birthday ever!"

She grinned up at Claire, very politely shook her hand and said, "Thank you." Then she turned back to her mother. "C'mon, Momma! Go! Go! Go!"

"Are you sure you'll be okay with George?" she said as Crista started dragging her out the door. "He can be a little... difficult sometimes."

"We'll be fine. Just take care of that beautiful daughter of yours. And don't worry. Difficult patients have always been my specialty."

DIE, YOU BASTARD! DIE!

ACKNOWLEDGEMENTS

Thanks to Jeff Borgio, the best little brother I never had for his EMS expertise.

My enormous and undying gratitude to the legendary John Skipp for his editorial skill, writerly talents and generous nature, I could never have finished this book without his unending energy and support.

Last, but not least, thanks to my husband Peter and my stepson Stephen for their love, support and cheerleading. It meant the world to me.

Jan Kozlowski is a freelance writer, editor and researcher. Her short horror stories have appeared in HUNGRY FOR YOUR LOVE: An Anthology of Zombie Romance and FANG-BANGERS: An Erotic Anthology of Fangs, Claws, Sex and Love, both edited by Lori Perkins; NECON EBOOKS FLASH FICTION ANTHOLOGY BEST OF 2011 edited by Matt Bechtel & Bob Booth; and WEIRD NOIR and NOIR CARNI-VAL edited by Kate Laity.

She lives in CT with her husband of 26 years, a neurotic German shepherd and 6 rescue cats.

Visit her website at *jankozlowski.com*